The Amethyst Summer

THE
AMETHYST SUMMER

by

BIANCA BRADBURY

IVES WASHBURN, INC.
NEW YORK

THE AMETHYST SUMMER

COPYRIGHT © 1963 BY BIANCA BRADBURY

LIBRARY OF CONGRESS CATALOG CARD NUMBER: 63-12146
MANUFACTURED IN THE UNITED STATES OF AMERICA

The Amethyst Summer

I

I was a hot June night. All the windows were open, and the only light in the comfortable living room of the Hughes house was the greenish face of the television set. For once, Bayley and her father were alone. Usually the house was swarming with brothers.

Mr. Hughes leaned back, watching a cops-and-robbers show. Happy, the basset hound, snored on his hassock within easy reach of his master's hand. Bayley's father sighed with pleasure. "This is a bit of all right," he said. "How come? To what are we indebted for this unnatural hush?"

"Tom's out on a date," Bayley reminded him. "Don't you remember? He borrowed your car. Benjy's in the garage taking his starter apart. I think Chip's in his room. I heard some of his pals clumping up the back stairs a while ago."

"Chip can't be in his room," her father stated, "because his record player isn't going."

"Maybe it broke," Bayley said.

A hopeful smile lit her father's face. "Maybe it did. We don't want to get our hopes up, Bayley, but . . ."

A trumpet wail, rising note on wobbly note, shattered that rosy dream. Mr. Hughes tensed. "He's got a new record," he muttered. "Bayley, that is an unbelievably awful sound."

Now a drum started an uncertain rhythm, and a deep bass boom-boom-boom accompanied it. A suspicion too horrible to voice crossed Bayley's mind.

"That's not a record." Her father said it for her. "No reputable music company would sell anything as terrible as that. There's something funny going on in this house."

"Well," Bayley said reluctantly, "it seems to me I heard that Tim Healy's parents gave him a bass fiddle for Christmas last year. And I think the other boy is Chip's pal, good old Charlie Morse, and Charlie plays trumpet in the high-school orchestra."

"And in a misguided moment we gave your brother a set of drums," her father finished. "Bayley, that boy beats me. We've only lived here six months, but already he has collected a gang to play baseball with and a gang to collect stamps with. Now it seems he's acquired a bunch of embryo musicians."

Bayley turned the television's volume higher, but now the trumpet was blatting out something that sounded vaguely like "Chinatown." Nothing could drown out the racket. "Bayley, go up and reconnoiter," her father ordered.

Bayley went upstairs. Chip's door was shut, and she listened outside. She heard Chip happily announce, "That was great. We all finished together."

She didn't wait to hear more, but crept downstairs to report to her father. "Dad," she said, "I hate to tell you, but those are humans up there, making the noises. It's Chip and Tim and Charlie Morse, and it's a jazz combo."

Her father seemed to shrivel in his chair, for the racket had started again, and this time the trumpet was blaring "I'm Looking Over a Four-Leaf Clover" with a fair amount of assurance. "After all," Bayley reminded him, "you were the one who bought Chip the drums."

"If your mother was home she'd do something about this," Mr. Hughes said.

Bayley's mother was in Brentford, where the Hughes family had lived until a few months earlier. She was going to be away for weeks, if not for months. Her Aunt Bayley, for whom Bayley was named, had broken her hip. This old lady was the family's favorite relative. She had raised her sister's child, after Bayley's mother had lost her own parents. The family had had no choice except to let their wife and mother go, for as long as she was needed.

Now Bayley said sensibly, "Dad, you know perfectly well what Mother would do. She'd say, 'Oh, isn't this just lovely, Chip's going to be a great drum player.' She'd march out to the kitchen and make a batch of brownies and feed those—those—"

"Oafs?" her father suggested.

"You know Mother. All her ducklings are swans."

Bayley realized that Benjy was leaning at the door. Of all her brothers, naturally she felt closest to this twin.

3

They looked so much alike that when she looked at him it was like seeing herself in a mirror, the same too thin, wiry body, the same russet hair, the same gray eyes. Benjy had a crew cut and her hair, although short, was brushed back, and that was about the only difference.

Now Benjy's face was dark. "What's that horrible racket above decks?" he demanded.

"Our brother's putting together a jazz combo," she informed him.

"Not in this house!" he bellowed.

The amateur musicians were now pounding out the beat with their feet, and the house began to shake. Mr. Hughes shot out of his chair. "They'll bring the ceiling down on us!" He stalked to the stairs. "Chip, come down here!"

"Dad, remember it's his home, too," Bayley said.

Her father took note of the warning, and his tone was reasonable when Chip called, "You want me, Dad?"

"Yes, son. We don't intend to discourage genius, but don't you think you've had enough for one night? We have to think of the neighbors, too. And when you beat your feet that way the whole house shakes."

"But Dad, we have to practice somewhere."

Benjy put in, "Your pals have homes, too, don't they? Or maybe they just crawl out of the woodwork."

"Shut up," Bayley ordered. One of her mother's precious rules was that the children's friends were welcome at any time, and this summer, while Bayley was taking her mother's place, she intended to run the house according to her mother's rules.

"Chip," she called, "if you'll come down, I'll make some sandwiches. And next time maybe you can do your practicing down-cellar. We'll clean it up and make it nice."

"Okay." Chip had such a sunny disposition that it was hard to hurt his feelings. "Come on down, gang," he yelled. "Bay's going to feed us."

"Hold on, small fry," Benjy interrupted. "Bay's got to help me in the garage. I want her to try the starter while I regulate the choke."

"That can wait," Bayley said.

"Why should it? Why do I have to wait while you feed those squirts?"

"I'll tell you why," Bayley said in a low voice, so that her youngest brother wouldn't hear. "We've got to keep them away from those instruments, because if they start playing again Dad's going to flip."

"Okay," Benjy agreed grudgingly.

She laid out slices of bread and began slathering half with peanut butter, the other half with jelly. The sight of food aroused her twin's appetite, and he began rummaging in the refrigerator. She snatched away the sliced ham just in time. It was being saved for her father's and Tom's lunches. With a sinking heart, Bayley realized that the refrigerator was getting perilously empty. Was it possible, she wondered, that her mother had been gone

5

only three days? She put together a sandwich for Benjy, rescued the last bottle of milk, and poured him a glass of root beer instead.

Chip and his pals were hunched over their sandwiches, discussing their musical career. Mr. Hughes had wandered back to his TV program. Benjy lounged against the sink. "Where's Happy?" he asked.

That was it. For some time, Bayley had been vaguely aware that something was wrong in the house. Usually, when anyone laid a hand on the refrigerator door, Happy came galumphing to get his handout. "You forgot to hook the screen door," she accused her twin.

"Why do you always blame me?" Benjy grumbled. But he put down his glass, and soon Bayley heard him out in the dark yard calling, "Come on, Happy. Good dog. Confound it! Where are you, you blasted dog?"

Suddenly, Bayley was overcome by a desire to be alone. She tiptoed up the back stairs, to get away from the musicians, from Benjy, from the sound of the television, where evidently the good guys had the bad guys cornered, because the rapid firing of guns filled the house.

She shut her door and leaned against it without putting on the light. This was her one haven in the whole house. She didn't feel like crying, although loneliness for her mother was a dull pain in her breast. She just felt like holding her hot face against the cool wood of the door. Exhaustion, from the long day of cleaning and cooking and keeping up with four men, had caught up with her. She felt tired to the marrow of her bones. How does

6

Mother do it? she wondered. How does Mother keep up with it year after year?

Then she thought: I hate men. It seemed as though, in a house crowded with three brothers and a father, she couldn't breathe.

Why couldn't we at least have a girl dog? she wondered. No, Happy was a male, too, and this very minute was off lady-chasing. If Benjy didn't find him soon, they would have to start combing the neighborhood. Happy was a darling and they adored him, but he was empty headed and irresponsible. Being a hound, he was a roamer.

Twice, since they had moved to Fenfield, Happy had been picked up by the dog warden. Once, while they were still living in Brentford, he had been carried home crying and bloody, with his hindquarters full of buckshot. The irate owner of a female dog had been driven to desperation by his lovesick baying and had let fly with a shotgun.

Bayley put on her light and powdered her nose. She had to go down and start coping again. She put on a cheerful expression for her father's sake. He was having a hard enough time as it was. He and her mother had been married for over twenty years, and this was the first time they had been separated. He was hiding his dismay as well as he could, but his temper was getting a little short, and when he learned that the dog was missing he might lose it.

Bayley started down. She had almost reached the foot of the stairs when a hand clutched her ankle. She should have been ready for it; living with three brothers, she had learned to brace herself against sudden clutchings and affectionate punches. This time Benjy caught her by surprise, and she pitched forward and landed in a heap.

Benjy rushed to help her up, but she was so mad she swung at him, and her hand caught the side of his face and she slapped him hard.

Roughly, he yanked her to her feet. He was angry, too, but more surprised than mad. "What's the matter with you?"

"Why don't you grow up?" she snapped back.

"Why didn't you grab the railing? Are you turning into one of those females who are always falling down and yelling?"

She knew what really ailed Benjy. He was afraid she was hurt, and he couldn't show his concern, so he had to sound angry. Bayley pushed him away and felt her arms and legs to make sure no bones were broken. "Don't you ever do that again as long as you live," she said with dignity.

"Okay, okay." The fight was over.

He went on, "That dog is really gone. Tom's got Dad's car, so we'll have to use mine, but first you'll have to hold the flashlight so I can connect up the starter rod."

The late news had finished. "I thought you kids were in bed," their father remarked, meeting them in the hall. "Where's Happy?"

"He's outside," Bayley said vaguely. "We'll be up in a minute."

8

"Good night." Mr. Hughes's tired feet carried him upstairs to his lonely room.

Bayley herself almost fell asleep as she leaned on the fender, holding the beam of light on the motor while her brother worked over it. She got behind the wheel to steer, and Benjy pushed the car out of the garage and down the drive, so that the sputter of the engine wouldn't call their father to his window. When they reached the street, she slid over and Benjy started the motor.

They drove along Greenwood Street and turned into the campus of the university, stopping often to listen for Happy's deep bark. The campus was dark and empty.

It was a lonesome thing to be doing, looking for a lost dog in the night. Bayley huddled forlornly on her side of the seat. Everybody loved Happy, but their mother loved him most. How could they tell her he was lost? She was planning to telephone the next evening, to find out how they were getting along.

They circled the neighborhood for an hour, up and down the streets. Officer Clancy was putting in a call at the police box on Willow Street when they came along, and they stopped. He said, "You're the Hughes kids, aren't you? I suppose you're dog-hunting again. If I see him, I'll return him. Go home now. It's late."

Benjy drove once more through the campus and turned into Greenwood Street. Tom was pulling into the drive. He opened the car door and hauled out a big bundle of dog. "I presume this is what you're looking for," he said.

He carried Happy in, to prevent him from scooting

9

off again in search of his lady friend. Happy flung himself at Bayley, but she pushed him away. "Aren't you going to feed him?" Tom asked.

"No," she muttered. "I hate dogs. I'm going to bed."

She told herself, as she climbed the stairs for the last time in a long, long day: I wish I had a female cat. Then I wouldn't be so alone in this awful, awful house. Why did they have to put so many men on this earth?

II

BAYLEY OPENED her eyes the next morning to a day of brilliant June sun. She should have awakened full of enthusiasm, but she felt no bounce at all.

The long, wonderful vacation was starting, and what would have happened ordinarily? Well, by time-honored custom, her mother would have brought her breakfast in bed. It was a family ritual, that during Bayley's first week of vacation she could sleep as late as she liked, that her mother would bring her a tray of coffee and toast. To the boys' annual protests that she made a slave of herself, Mrs. Hughes would have said, "I've only got one daughter, so I guess I can treat her like a princess once in a while if I want to."

Was it only three days ago that the call had come from the hospital in Brentford, a hundred miles away? Aunt Bayley's doctor made no bones about her need. "You're all she's got, Elizabeth, so I guess you'll have to come."

"Of course I'll come," Mrs. Hughes assured him. "I'll get there as soon as I can, and I'll stay as long as she needs me."

A family council took place. Nobody questioned Mrs.

Hughes's decision, although her husband's face grew longer and longer as he realized how many weeks she might be away. "Bayley will take my place here," Mrs. Hughes said.

"That's great, Mom! Of course I will." Bayley felt noble and at the same time proud of her mother's confidence in her.

"You'll all help your sister, won't you?"

"Sure, we'll manage just fine," Tom had told her positively.

"You mean old Bayley's going to take care of us?" Chip's tone was plaintive. Benjy punched him to shut him up.

Their mother spent an entire day filling the refrigerator, the cake box, the cookie jar. Bayley tagged at her heels while she explained the hundreds of things Bayley must know about running a house.

Bayley was aghast now, remembering how confidently she had promised, "I'll manage okay. There's nothing to it. Don't you give the house or us another thought, Mom."

Her mother hadn't been so easily reassured. "I wish now I hadn't let you grow up such a tomboy," she fretted. "You were always wonderful about helping around the house, Bayley, but I should have made you take more responsibility. Now I'm not even sure you can get a simple meal on the table."

" I still say there's nothing to it," Bayley said blithely.

"It was so much easier for me to run the house, I made

the mistake of not insisting that you learn," her mother went on. "Now you'll have to learn it all the hard way. You're going to have the wits scared out of you, for instance, when you find out how much the men eat. They all have hollow legs.

"Another thing," she continued, "don't let them run roughshod over you. Stand up for your rights and make them help."

"I will. They'll do their share."

"We've lived in Fenfield such a short time, I don't know any older woman you can turn to, if you need help or advice."

The important thing, Bayley knew, was that her mother go away with an easy mind about affairs at home. "You're not to worry," she said firmly.

"Your biggest job will be taking care of your dad. Bayley, I panic when I think of leaving him. You kids will scratch along somehow, but he'll be so lonesome he won't know what to do. Keep him company as much as you can."

She was still issuing instructions when they drove her to the train. Tom and Mr. Hughes stowed her suitcase and settled her in her seat. The last thing she called through the train window was, "Bayley, you make the men toe the line and behave themselves, hear?"

Now the sun said seven o'clock and Bayley tensed, waiting for the shrill yell of the alarm clock. It shattered the silence, and she heard her father groan as he reached out to turn it off. Down the hall, Tom's bed squeaked.

Tom was working at the paper factory this summer, between his sophomore and junior years at the university, and his shift started at eight. Benjy, too, if Bayley remembered her twin's schedule right, had to get to the supermarket early. He was working in order to support his beloved car. Only Chip was free to sleep on blissfully, while the rest of the family launched the morning attack on the bathroom.

The men were converging on it when Bayley shot by them and slammed the door. "I have to go first because I have to cook your breakfasts!" she shouted.

She washed sketchily and brushed her teeth. When she came out, the three were leaning against the wall, somberly regarding her. "A pretty-looking crew you are," she commented.

She yanked on blue jeans and an old shirt and ran downstairs. Happy, hysterical with joy that another wonderful day had begun, leaped from the sofa to knock her down. She wrestled him out the back door and tied him on his rope.

In the few days her mother had been away, Bayley had mastered the mysteries of the percolator, and she soon had the coffee perking. She poured orange juice and slapped plates and silver on the kitchen table. How did her mother manage to set a neat table so early in the morning? she wondered.

She then surveyed the refrigerator. There was one egg, and no bacon. She knew beyond the shadow of a doubt that this was the day all the men would come charging through the door demanding bacon and eggs.

She boiled the egg for her father. Four minutes seemed a reasonable length of time. Then she busied herself with making toast.

When she turned around, Benjy had slid into his place and was just about to crack the egg with his knife. Bayley snatched it back just in time. "That's Pa's!"

"Where's mine?"

"You don't get one. You can have dry cereal."

"I hate dry cereal."

"You'll eat dry cereal and like it."

A man's large hand caught her mop of hair and swung her around. Tom, like Benjy, was used to handling Bayley as though she were a sack of meal, and no yelps or show of wounded dignity could discourage him. Bayley kicked at him, and he let her go. "Where's my bacon and eggs?" he asked mildly.

"You'll eat dry cereal, too, and like it!"

"Look here, Carrots," Tom said, "you're supposed to keep the place stocked up. I can't do a day's work on bird food. You can make me some oatmeal this morning, but after this I want bacon and eggs."

Their father came in then. He took in the chaos in the kitchen at a glance, saw that Bayley was beleaguered by her brothers, and suggested, "Your sister's doing her best, so let's give her a chance to learn her job before we pitch into her."

Mollified, Bayley served him first. Then she threw oatmeal on top of boiling water. It cohered in a lumpy mess. Tom poked at it with a spoon, then pushed it away and contented himself with toast and coffee.

Tom was the one brother Bayley counted on to be tolerant and reasonable, and his cavalier treatment of the oatmeal stung her. She was too busy, however, making sandwiches and packing them in lunch boxes to renew the battle.

Benjy lingered after the others had left. If Bayley expected any sympathy from her twin, however, she was disappointed again. "You've got nothing to do but hang around the house," he commented. "You ought to try heaving those heavy cartons around, and bagging groceries for eight hours at a stretch. Then you'd find out you've really got a snap."

She glowered after him as he departed for his day's work.

Now at last she had the house to herself, except for Chip. She wandered upstairs. She had to begin somewhere, so she started with her father's room. She ripped off sheets and pillowcases and tossed them down the back stairs and made his bed. She hung up his pajamas and straightened the shoes in his closet. One room done.

She soon lost her ambition to change all the sheets, and tidied Tom's bed with a few impatient tugs. Who did he think he was? she thought. He didn't deserve clean linen. She started to hang up his clothes, but when his coat promptly slid off the hanger she left it where it lay.

16

She opened the bathroom door, yipped, "Oh, no!" and slammed it shut. However, no matter how bad the shambles was, she had to tackle it. Her disgust with men mounted as she scoured the bowl and tub, hung up fresh towels, retrieved the cap of the toothpaste and wadded the soiled towels in a large, wet ball.

She couldn't believe they would dare leave the bathroom in such a state if her mother was home. Were they trying her out, to see how far they could push her?

She made her own bed, and at last combed her hair. Then she went to Chip's and Benjy's room. For a moment, the sight of Chip's seraphic face softened her. He looked almost angelic when he was sleeping. But then she thought, what right does he have to sleep when I'm working so hard? He ought to be helping me. She gave the lump in the bed a resounding whack.

Chip roused up with a roar. "What's the matter with you? Why do you have to act so mean? You've ruined my day!"

"I'll ruin your day for you if you don't get up," she said severely. "You're suppose to be helping me. Rise and shine!"

She marched downstairs, kicking the pile of dirty clothes ahead of her. She gathered it into a heap again and tossed it down the cellar stairs. She would cope with it later. Now Happy was baying in the back yard.

His rope had tangled around the power mower, which Benjy had abandoned in the middle of the lawn the day before. But that wasn't what ailed Happy. What made him yelp and quiver with joy was the sight of a furniture van, which was backing up to the white house next door, beyond the privet hedge.

This place had stood empty ever since the Hughes family had moved into theirs. It belonged to the university, Bayley knew. She guessed that a new member of the faculty must be arriving.

Chip, buttoning his pants around his skinny waist, had come up behind her. "Hey, we've got new neighbors! Maybe they've got some kids my age."

"If there's one thing we don't need around here, it's more boys," Bayley told him. "Maybe they've got girls. We could certainly use some girls."

A stout, gray-haired man of about her father's age was standing on the front porch, directing the movers. A hi-fi set went in, then several cases of books. "He's a teacher, that's for sure," Bayley observed.

"Where are the kids?" Chip wanted to know.

An upstairs window opened, and a dark-haired boy, wearing spectacles, leaned out. "Do you need me down there, Father?" he called.

"Yes," his father answered. "Come and tell us where you want your boxes of specimens to go."

"Specimens," Chip mused. "What kind of specimens? Butterflies? That's all we need around here, somebody who collects butterflies. Ye gods!"

Bayley had lost interest. These two, and a woman she saw moving around in the kitchen, seemed to be the sum total of the new family, and they didn't look very exciting.

Chip followed her in, and poured the last of the milk over the last of the dry cereal. Bayley went to the telephone. Maybe the arrival of the new family was no world-shaking event, but at least she owed it to her only girl friend in Fenfield to let her know.

Jean Tolland answered promptly. "What's new?"

"Nothing much, except that some people have moved in next door." Bayley described the new arrivals.

Jean was immediately interested when she learned there was a boy. "What does he look like?"

"Eeek," Bayley said.

"Have you seen Jerry lately?" Jean was trying to promote the idea that Bayley ought to go steady with Jerry Flint, who was vice-president of their class in high school. So far, her scheming hadn't resulted in one single, solid date, much less a desire on Jerry's part to see Bayley as his steady girl.

"You know perfectly well I haven't seen Jerry; you'd have been the first to hear," Bayley told her.

Jean Tolland had two sisters and no brothers, so she had no idea what boys were really like. She considered them the most wonderful things that had developed since life had first emerged from the primeval ooze. "Maybe this youth who's moved in isn't so bad," she suggested. "What are you doing today, Bay? Maybe I'd better come over and take a look at him."

"I'm making beds and washing dishes, and then I've got to clean this entire doggone house."

"Isn't there anybody there to help you?" This was Jean's delicate way of finding out whether Benjy was home. Jean was between steadies, and looking around for a new one.

"Only Chip, and he's no help."

"We've got a date for this afternoon, anyway. Don't forget, we're going to give each other permanents. Have you got the stuff for yours?"

"No, but I'll get it when I go shopping this afternoon."

This was about all that was really consequential in the conversation, but when Bayley hung up and looked at the clock, she was surprised to discover that an hour had elapsed.

She dusted the downstairs, then hauled the vacuum cleaner out of the closet. She plugged in the cord, but all that happened was a small explosion and a puff of smoke. She yanked out the plug. "Chip!" she called.

Chip didn't answer. When she went to look for him, he had vanished.

By this time it was noon, and time to think about lunch. Bayley was a little startled to discover that during the course of her busy morning she had forgotten the breakfast dishes, which were still piled in the sink, and a discouraging mess they were. She washed them, scrubbed the sink, and, feeling noble because at least the kitchen was presentable, went upstairs.

As she passed Chip's room, she noticed that his bed was still a tangled mess. She started to pull it apart, and then changed her mind. She wasn't the servant in this house, the slavey who made the beds any old hour the lords and masters deigned to arise!

The supermarket was four blocks away. It was a pleasant sort of a thing to be doing, Bayley discovered, to be walking along the shady street to the store.

How many times had she accompanied her mother on marketing trips? Hundreds. Well, dozens, anyway. However, once she was inside, Bayley realized how little attention she had paid to how her mother shopped. The store, with aisles crowded with goods, was like an enormous maze. She took a cart and started piling in bread, butter, vegetables, helter-skelter.

Benjy was working in the dog-food section, stamping prices on cans. "Hello, Dopey," he greeted her. No matter how indifferent this twin tried to act, he couldn't keep his face from lighting up when he saw her. "What are you going to get for dinner? How about some pork chops?"

"Dad doesn't like them."

"How about some lamb chops, then?"

"Okay, we'll have lamb chops. What kind of food does Happy like?"

"How should I know?" Benjy asked. "You're the one who's running the house."

Bayley loaded up with several cans, figuring that if Happy didn't like what she chose he could jolly well make the best of it. She had enough problems trying to cater to human whims.

The display of cookies intrigued her, and she chose several kinds. They were low on peanut butter, and she located that. She happened to pass the coffee counter and remembered she had used the last for breakfast. The meat counter baffled her, but at least she knew a lamb chop when she saw one, and, although the price seemed high, she took several packages. Four men, she guessed, could put away an awful lot of lamb chops.

She chose different kinds of jam, several boxes of ice cream and a big jar of pickles. Her cart was piled high when she joined the line at one of the check-out counters.

Bayley's purchases filled four bags and took all her money. She was astonished to discover that she had spent fifteen dollars; a few dimes and pennies were all that were left in her purse.

Benjy was helping the girl at the cash register, and bagged the groceries for Bayley. She asked him, "Now, how do I get all this stuff home? I forgot to bring Mother's cart."

"That's your problem," he told her.

"Can't you carry it home for me?"

"No, of course not, Dopey. You think I can just walk out and take a stroll for myself?"

"I'll borrow one of the store carts, then. You can bring it back tomorrow."

"Oh yeah?" Benjy snorted. "You want me to get arrested because my sister steals store property?"

"So I have to walk four blocks home and four blocks back, to get Mother's?"

"It looks that way, sweetheart," Benjy assured her, bagging the next order, which was piling up in front of him.

Fuming, Bayley made the long trek home and back. Benjy obligingly packed the bags in their mother's light metal wagon, then pushed it across the street to help Bayley up the curb.

"Benjy, can you loan me five dollars?" she asked. "I haven't got a cent. Jean and I are going to give each other home permanents, and I have to get the stuff for mine at the drugstore."

"Listen," he said, "if I had five dollars I'd sit up all night and watch it."

How could life be so difficult? Bayley wondered, as she trundled her heavy groceries along the last, long block. She looked up and saw that Jean was already sitting on the front steps, waiting for her. They carried in the groceries. Then they retired to the bathroom.

This was the first time either of them had ever actually used a home-permanent kit. It was just as well, they soon discovered, that they had the equipment to do only one head. The process, which sounded so easy when you read the directions, became unexpectedly complicated. By the time they had done up Jean's flyaway, light hair on the curlers, applied the lotion, given her curls the neutralizer, washed her hair, and set it in pin curls, the afternoon was gone. The bathroom was once again a real shambles.

Mr. Hughes's tired step sounded in the front hall. "Oh murder," Bayley muttered, "here's Dad and I haven't even put the groceries away." She was so tired, and her arms ached so from working over her friend's head, that she slumped on the edge of the bathtub, reluctant to move.

Jean tied a scarf around her wet head. "I'll help you."

Tom, too, was just arriving. Luckily, it was Tom and not his father who fell over the vacuum cleaner, still sprawled across the living room. Bayley ignored his irate comments and made for the kitchen.

Mr. Hughes was just standing there, looking stunned. Bayley had been so absorbed in helping Jean with her beautifying, she had even forgotten to put the frozen food away. Ice cream had melted and flowed across the table, softening the bags. Dry cereal and vegetables and soap flakes and cookies were scattered over the floor.

Now Bayley realized that Happy had been quiet all afternoon, and she saw why. He had lapped up all the melted ice cream, then browsed through the rest of the food. He had eaten one package of chops. Luckily, having gorged himself, he had left the other packets of meat untouched.

Bayley yelled at sight of this horrible chaos, then swooped at Happy. He gazed at her with soulful eyes and wagged his tail. Then he heaved and was sick.

Jean backed away. "I just remembered my mother asked me to do some errands," she said. "I'm sorry, I've got to go." She vanished.

Chip opened the back door. "Holy cow," he breathed.

"Don't you open your big fat yap!" Bayley ordered fiercely. "Just take your dog out and tie him up."

She began to paw through the mess. Without a word,

her father and Tom went to work. With their help, the kitchen was soon clear, and Bayley could begin the dinner. The frozen peas had survived with little damage, and, after washing the ice cream off the potatoes and the surviving packages of lamb chops, she could put together a fairly attractive dinner. Meager, but attractive.

She fed the men in the dining room, to remove them from the scene of the recent disaster. Benjy slid into his place just as they were starting. Chip began to yap again because what he found on his plate was potato, peas, and a peanut-butter sandwich instead of chops. Bayley glared him down, and when he saw that she was making do with the same meal as his, he subsided.

Nobody ate much, and nobody spoke. "Would anybody like some nice canned peaches for dessert?" Bayley asked, but nobody seemed to care for any nice canned peaches. The telephone rang just as they were getting up, the horrible meal over.

"If that's your mother calling, don't one of you breathe a word of this," Mr. Hughes ordered. "As far as she's concerned, everything is fine at home. Do you understand? Not one word! Half of you go upstairs and get on the extension phone."

It was their mother's cheery voice on the line. A painful lump in Bayley's throat made it impossible for her to speak, but the boys asked how Aunt Bayley was, whether she was in pain, whether she was fussing about being in the hospital.

Bayley was sharing the downstairs phone with her

father. "Now tell me about things at home," her mother said.

The boys chorused, "Just fine. Don't worry about us, Mom."

"Did Bayley cook you a nice dinner tonight?"

There was a pause, and then Chip let out a strangled cry. Mr. Hughes said loudly, "Bayley cooked us a wonderful dinner."

"That's good," Mrs. Hughes said. "I knew she would turn into a fine little housekeeper. Well, dears, this call is costing money. I'll have to hang up, much as I hate to."

"Wait," Bayley begged. "Dad, will you and the others please get off the line and let me talk to Mother?"

The line clicked upstairs, and Mr. Hughes left Bayley alone. "Mother," Bayley whispered, "you ought to know the truth. Everything is simply incredibly awful. I'm the world's worst housekeeper. Mother, you'll just have to come home. Maybe we could swap. Maybe I could come to Brentford and take care of Aunt Bayley." She started to tell all the things that had gone wrong.

Her mother broke in, and Bayley could hardly believe her ears. Mrs. Hughes said calmly, "Don't tell me the bad news, dearest, because there's nothing I can do about it. I have no choice. I have to stay here. You'll have to do your best, and I know your best is pretty wonderful. Are the men helping you?"

"Yes, they're just fine." How could Bayley say one word against them, after the noble way they had carried on tonight?

26

"You'll soon get the hang of it, and things will begin to run smoothly. Good-bye now, dear."

"Mother, don't hang up!"

"I have to, dearest. Good-bye."

Unable to believe her ears, Bayley held the silent receiver. Her own mother had abandoned her.

The boys had scattered, but Mr. Hughes stayed to help clear the table and wipe the dishes. Drip, drip, drip, Bayley's tears plopped into the dish water. Her father clumsily hugged her when they finished. "Cheer up, daughter, we'll live through this, and believe it or not, the day will come when we'll laugh about it."

III

ONCE IN THE NIGHT Bayley jerked awake from a dream that she was being buried alive under a mountain of sheets, towels, and shirts, down whose sides slid endless dirty dishes. However, she arose feeling strong and virtuous and filled with good intentions, determined to turn over a new leaf. That was the lovely thing about the night. It was like a sponge that wiped a bad day clean from the slate.

This was Saturday morning, and Tom had the day off. Benjy was due at the market an hour later than usual. Their father planned to spend the day at his office. The move to Fenfield had meant an advancement for him in the oil company he worked for. An added inducement in Fenfield, of course, was the fact that Tom was attending the university, and in due course the twins and then Chip would follow in his footsteps. With four children to educate, the fact that they could live at home was an important advantage to Mr. Hughes.

Bayley flew downstairs to get her father's breakfast. When he came down he found the table set, the coffee made, and a cheerful daughter waiting for him. His face cleared and he looked almost happy, for the first time in several days.

Before he had a chance to speak Bayley told him, "Dad, I've let you down horribly, but you and the boys were wonderful last night when we were talking to Mother. Things are going to be different around here. I promise."

Mr. Hughes said earnestly, "Honey, we don't expect miracles. I'd be the first to admit that your mother has spoiled us all. She's a tiptop housekeeper. Maybe she slipped up, not teaching you how to do things. I suppose it was easier for her to do them herself, because she's so efficient."

He chuckled. "I bet she never told you this. She had to learn her job from scratch, too. When we were married somebody gave us a sandwich toaster as a wedding present, and for the first month your mother fed me toasted cheese sandwiches every night. I got so sick of cheese sandwiches, I used to stop at a restaurant on my way home from work, and fortify myself with a good meal. She found out, and we had an awful row. She saw the light, though, and started reading cookbooks. Things began looking up, and she turned into a first-class cook. Some time, though, I'll mention toasted cheese sandwiches, and you watch how red she gets. She won't admit she tried to starve me to death, but it's the solemn truth."

He left for work, and Bayley energetically began to clean house. Tom or Benjy would have to fix the vacuum-cleaner cord for her, but while they were still sleeping she dusted and tidied the downstairs, and watered all fifty pots of her mother's African violets, lined up on the shelves that filled one wall of the dining room. Some looked wilted, but remembering her mother's instructions: "They don't like wet feet. They'd rather be too dry than too wet," Bayley was careful not to overwater them.

She was arranging the pots artistically when Tom came yawning down. "Hi," he said. "Where's my white sweater?"

"I don't know."

"It was with a pile of stuff on my chair."

"It went down with the laundry, then."

"It's supposed to go to the cleaners," he said, "but I need it today. Beth and I are going for a picnic on the river."

Bayley heard him start down-cellar, then bellow, "Ye gods! Bay!"

"What's the matter now?" she called.

"Look at what you've done! You just threw the stuff down the stairs, and somebody, I suppose it was Chip, clumped up and down wiping his big feet all over everything."

Bayley didn't blame him for being angry. Beth Somers had knitted this sweater for him. Tom was head over heels in love with Beth, so the sweater she had made with her own lily-white hands was sacred to him. "Tom, I'm awfully sorry," Bayley began.

"What good is sorry?" he snorted. "This looks like tar!"

"It's not tar, it's just plain dirt. I'll pay for having it cleaned."

"That's not the point," Tom said. "The point is that you don't think. Look at the sheets and towels! Oh, Chip did a good job when he was kicking them around. Mother never simply tossed the stuff down the stairs, but 'Out of sight, out of mind,' that's your motto."

Despite her good intentions to be pleasant, Bayley felt rage swelling in her breast, and she said, "If I couldn't knit a better sweater than that, I'd give up."

Maybe there was jealousy mixed with her anger. When she was a little girl, Tom had been Bayley's special pal. Tom had defended her against her twin's violent onslaughts. Tom had taught her to play tennis and swim a good crawl stroke. In return, Bayley had given this oldest of her brothers blind adoration.

He had gone off to college and then Beth had come into his life. After that, nobody except Beth had received any real attention from him.

Once Mrs. Hughes had caught Bayley working up a temper because Tom had broken a date to take her to a movie. "That silly Beth just crooks her finger and off he runs," Bayley had fumed.

"That's the way life is," her mother had told her, "and it's natural. You'd like Beth if she wasn't so important in Tom's life now. Don't show it when you feel jealous," her mother had warned. "You won't gain a thing, and you'll lose the lovely feeling you and Tom have always had for each other."

Well, there certainly wasn't any lovely feeling between them this morning. Tom snatched the sweater from her and started out the door. "Aren't you even going to wait for your breakfast?" Bayley called after him.

He stopped on the front steps, then came back. "I'm sorry," he growled.

"I'm sorry, too," Bayley admitted. "That was a lousy thing I said. It's a wonderful sweater."

"Okay, let's skip it. I've got to go and get my car."

"What's the matter with it?"

"It's at the gas station being washed."

Bayley thought, He even has to have his stupid car washed and polished so Beth can ride in it. But she kept this to herself. Trying to be friendly to match Tom's friendliness, she suggested, "You can bring Beth home for dinner if you want to."

Despite himself, Tom shuddered at this suggestion, but said politely, "Thanks just the same, Sis, but Beth is fixing a picnic. We'll be gone all day. Take it easy, now. Have fun, kid."

Have fun, wow! Have yourself a ball, kid. After you make the beds and wash the dishes, you can have a jolly time coping with all that laundry.

She was stuffing clothes into the machine when Benjy called from the top of the cellar stairs, "Hey, what are you doing down there?"

"I'm loading the washer."

"Did you get it fixed?"

"No. What's the matter with it?"

"Don't you remember, Dopey? Almost the last thing

32

Mother said was to call the appliance store and have the man come, because it's busted. It's probably the timing. Maybe if I take the back off I can see what's wrong."

"No," Bayley said firmly, "don't you lay one single pinky on Mother's machine. If you're such a mechanical genius, maybe you can fix the vacuum-cleaner cord, but don't you touch the washer."

She called the store, and the man promised to come the next week. "So now I'm stuck with a cellar full of dirty clothes," she told Benjy. "And when I say dirty I mean dirty. Chip used them to wipe his feet on. I'll have to take them to the laundromat."

"Here comes your love-life," Benjy mentioned, hearing a commotion in the yard. Happy was wildly lunging at a boy who had stopped to pet him.

"How's my favorite basset hound?" Jerry Flint asked, grabbing Happy's long ears and tying them on top of the dog's head.

Bayley's grumpiness vanished like dew before the morning sun. Maybe Jerry Flint wasn't exactly her love-life, but he could be any time he took the notion.

Watching him wrestling with Happy, however, Bayley began to feel nervous. Why was it that when a boy came to the house she felt so stupid and clumsy, all knobby knees and elbows? Why was she afraid to open her mouth for fear the wrong remark would pop out?

Jean couldn't understand it. "You've grown up with three brothers," she pointed out. "You ought to know how to handle men by now."

It was this having three brothers that hurt her chances

33

with other boys, Bayley suspected. In Brentford, she had grown up in a house that was overrun with males, males who had nothing on their minds but football or baseball or praticing basketball shots. What used to happen in those days? Tom or Benjy or Chip would say, "Come on, Bay, we need you." In self-defense, Bayley had learned to bat out runs if it was baseball, to run interference and try to get herself killed if it was football, to throw baskets as well as any of them. This hadn't been exactly a hardship. She had always like boys' sports.

So what happened when they moved to Fenfield? Her mother had seen the problem clearly. "Moving to a new town will be good for you, Bayley," she had said. "We'll make a new start. You're too old to be a tomboy any longer, dear."

But before Bayley had a chance to establish the fact that she wasn't a hopeless case as a female, the same pattern began to repeat itself. Tom brought home classmates from the university; Benjy brought home his pals. They got out the ball and bat. "Bay will catch for us," they said.

Bayley went on strike. When they said, "Good old Bay will catch for us," good old Bay said, "No."

"You sick or something?" they asked then.

"No, I'm not sick," she said.

After that, they ignored her.

Jerry was the only boy who sometimes hung around and talked. He was an only child, and gravitated towards the Hughes house, with its big yard and dog and boys, as though it were a magnet. With his shining, dark hair and even features, he was extremely good-looking. Bayley was used to bristly crew cuts, and often thought she would like to find out what silky hair felt like.

Now Bayley said, "Hi," and he said, "Hi." There the conversation died.

At least, Bayley could be thankful she had put on her decent green shorts and a girl's blouse this morning. Jerry wasn't finding her looking as though she'd been put together out of a ragbag.

"I suppose you're looking for Benjy," she said. She meant it to sound coy, implying, "Here's little old me. Won't I do?" Instead, it sounded gruff and ungracious.

"No, not particularly. Where is he?"

"He's gone to work."

"What are you doing?" Jerry inquired.

"I've got to cope with the wash. I suppose I'll have to haul it over to the laundromat."

"I'll take you. My car's in front."

"Oh, no," Bayley said quickly, "you don't want to do that." Right away, she could have bitten her tongue out. It did seem awfully inappropriate that Jerry's neat convertible should be used to carry dirty clothes, but Jean would have handled the situation better. Jean would have worked it so that she and the laundry would be riding around in Jerry's car.

"Okay, suit yourself," Jerry shrugged.

Bayley wrestled Chip's wooden wagon out from behind Benjy's car in the garage, getting herself dirty in

35

the process, getting madder by the minute. Chip came along just as she succeeded in yanking it free. He seemed pleased by the sight of this old wagon, which he hadn't played with for years, and took a rag and wiped it clean.

"What's to eat?" he asked, but Bayley knew the inquiry was purely a reflex. When Chip's conscious mind wasn't thinking about food, his unconscious mind took over and went right on working on the problem.

"I'll fix lunch when I get home," she said.

Chip just stood and watched when she came out of the house, staggering under two pillowcases stuffed to overflowing. Jerry's good manners got the better of him. He took her bundles, remarking, "Whether you want to ride in my car or not, I'm taking you."

Thus, no thanks to Bayley, things worked out better than she had dared to hope. She wished that some of her high-school acquaintances could see her in Jerry's car, but who was on the streets at noon on a Saturday? Nobody who mattered.

She tried to make chitchat with Jerry, but what came out? "How many cylinders does this thing have?" Wasn't that a romantic-type remark?

However, Jerry didn't abandon her when they reached the laundromat. This was lucky, because Bayley had forgotten her purse. Jerry fed quarters into two empty machines. The women who were wating for their own washes to get done looked up from their magazines and smiled.

"We can't wait here," Jerry said. "Come on." He

marched Bayley to Harper's Drugstore and bought her a soda. Soon, they went back and transferred the clothes to a drier, then returned for another soda.

With all the soda sloshing around inside her, Bayley wasn't particularly interested in food when they got back to the house. Chip was, however. He was taking the lawn mower apart, and when they drove in, he sprawled on the grass and started to moan.

"What's the matter with you?" Bayley demanded, falling into the trap.

"I'm dying. Get me food," he gasped.

"Come on in," Bayley ordered Jerry. Any hopes she'd had of building up a romantic situation were gone now. Chip was acting his worst. She still owed Jerry at least some lunch, though, for his kindness.

Benjy arrived while she was frying bacon. Soon Bayley found herself wallowing in a sea of lettuce and sliced tomatoes. Bread was spread in rows as though she was feeding an army. Her brothers and an enthusiastic Jerry began banging spoons, demanding speed.

Mrs. Hughes had said all boys had hollow legs, and Bayley was learning this was true. She wondered now if her mother ever got this feeling of desperation, trying to fill their bottomless stomachs.

Chip got a strangle hold on the conversation. It seemed he had used his morning to find out about the people who had moved next door. "Their last name is Sudak, or something like that," he said. "I think the father is a big shot, but I don't know what kind. I just talked to the long drink of water with the glasses. They've got a yellow cat. It came into our yard and Happy cornered it, and this guy came over to rescue it. His name's Bruno. He's about six feet tall."

"Aren't there any girls?" Bayley asked.

"Yeah. It's funny—he's got a twin sister. I told him about you and Benjy, and that it seemed pretty queer, their moving in next door and each family having a set of twins. And if that wasn't funny enough, they'll be in the same class with you and Benjy. They'll be juniors next year."

"Did you see the sister?" Bayley wanted to know.

"No. That was another screwy thing. This Bruno and I were sitting under the forsythia. He was holding his cat and I was holding Happy, and we were chewing the fat. But all the time the mother was standing in a window, watching. She seemed really worried. Finally, I said to Bruno, 'Your mother wants you for something.'

"She came to the door then and called him. He answered her in German or Russian or something."

"How about Polish?" Benjy asked.

"Maybe. Anyway, this Bruno jumped to his feet and answered her in the same lingo, and then he said, 'I'm sorry, my mother is nervous about strangers. I'll have to go in.'

"I said, 'Heck, I'm not a stranger. I live next door.' "

"Did you like him?" Bayley wanted to know. Because the Hughes family, too, was new in Fenfield, she felt immediate sympathy for the Sudaks. It was not an easy thing to start a new life in a new school, in a new town.

"Sudak," Jerry mused. "I remember reading something in the paper about him last winter. It was a big thing that the university got him to come here. I think he's the new head of the chemistry department."

Of course, the minute lunch was over Benjy and Chip started to decamp. Bayley forgot the dignity she was trying to maintain in front of Jerry, and collared Chip. "I know you," she said, glaring at him. "You'd skin out like a rat leaving the sinking ship. Before Dad gets home, you're going to finish the lawn. I don't want any ifs, ands, or buts. You've had fun taking the mower apart, so now you can have fun putting it together again."

Pausing occasionally to glare at the house, Chip got the mower working. He stuck with the job. Bayley had set up the ironing board and tackled the clean clothes. Boys aren't all bad, she admitted. They're pretty awful, but they've got a few redeeming virtues.

Jerry wandered back and forth, taking turns with Chip for a go around the yard with the mower, returning to the kitchen to watch Bayley iron. However, he eventually grew bored with watching them slaving, and announced abruptly, "I've got to go," and got up and went.

The mound of clothes looked as high as the Alps or something. Each individual sheet meant a battle before it was folded. The rack was soon full, and Bayley began festooning the ironed pieces over doors. The kitchen began to smell like a Chinese laundry. The heat rose. It was a warm afternoon in Fenfield, and the hottest place in Fenfield was the Hughes kitchen.

Bayley had saved the hardest pieces until the last—the men's dress shirts and her own blouses. There were six shirts. Bayley had not the slightest idea how to iron them, but she did her best. Each one took twenty minutes.

The shadows lengthened. The lawn was finished, and Chip had long since disappeared, but Bayley was still struggling with her job. Exhausted, she flung the last piece down on the ironing board. It was her best white blouse. Just as the iron descended she remembered: It's drip-dry. There was a horrible smell, a sizzling, and the front of the blouse came off on the iron. The synthetic fabric bubbled disgustingly. The electric iron was a mess.

Bayley could have yelled with helpless rage or else dissolved in tears, but she did neither. She calmly wadded the blouse into a ball and stuffed it in the garbage can and set the iron on the drainboard to cool.

She heard her father at the front door, and when he came in search of her, his face was full of apprehension. It cleared when he saw her own look of false serenity. "Hello, dear," he said. "How about a cool drink for your old man? What time are we having dinner? Did you have a nice day?"

Bayley swallowed and counted to ten and told him, "I had a lovely day, Daddy. I had a simply peachy day."

IV

WELL, it was Sunday. Sunday had actually arrived, and for once Bayley found herself with a free hour on her hands. Furthermore, not one of her men was going to bellow, "Bayley, what have we got to eat?" Their stomachs were stuffed full of roast beef and baked potatoes and string beans, and it had been good, if Bayley did say so herself as shouldn't. As a matter of fact, her tribe had been so appreciative, they had stuck around to help clean up the dishes.

So now she had retired to the back yard and a lawn chair hidden under the droopy willow tree.

Her father was the only one at home, and Bayley supposed he was napping. Poor Dad had looked forward to quite a different kind of Sunday. At breakfast he had announced, "We're all going to Brentford and take your mother out to dinner." Then he had put through a call to his wife, to let her know.

Mrs. Hughes hadn't answered at Aunt Bayley's apartment, and he had called the hospital. When she came to the phone she sounded really woebegone. "Oh, darling, I'm sick about this," she had said. "You can't imagine how much I want to see you."

Bayley, listening on the extension, realized that her indomitable mother was fighting for control. "I can't get away even for an hour," she went on. "It wouldn't pay you to come over. Aunt Bayley had a bad night, and the hospital called me this morning to come right over. I don't think she's in any immediate danger, but she's having a great deal of pain. Of course, with a person her age they're always afraid of pneumonia or heart failure. She's no complainer, you know that, but it's a comfort to her if I stick close. You do understand, don't you, dears?"

"Of course we do," Mr. Hughes assured her. His wife's peace of mind was his chief concern.

"Ben, how are things at home?"

"Couldn't be better!"

"That's a relief." Bayley got the distinct impression that, although her mother was glad to hear that all was well, she actually felt very far away from them, removed from their problems.

Bayley had compiled quite a list of questions to ask when next she talked with her mother. There were so many things she didn't know about running a house! Today, she kept her questions to herself.

Her father had mastered his disappointment and had helped Bayley keep the house cheerful. Now he was upstairs taking his nap. He always said he went up to think, but his family couldn't help noticing that, almost as soon as he lay down to do his Sunday thinking, his book hit his nose and his gentle snores reverberated through the house.

Happy whined, and Bayley went to see what ailed him. As usual, he had tangled his rope around the rhododendrons and woven it in and out among the garden tools leaning against the porch. A spade banged against him when he tried to move.

He got into this kind of trouble a dozen times a day, and Bayley had announced only that morning, "If we could hire help, I wouldn't want a maid. I'd just have a man in a fancy uniform who did nothing all day except untangle that hound." Now, because she really adored Happy, she said, "You poor beast, you hate to be tied, but if you had a grain of brains inside your head you wouldn't run away."

As he always did, Happy leaped on her to express his gratitude. This time, he succeeded in knocking her down, to kiss her and wipe his smelly long ears across her face. Although he was low-slung, he was an extremely powerful dog. Bayley threw him away from her. She was developing muscles like a lady Atlas, wrestling sixty pounds of adoring dog. She fought her way free and started unraveling the web of rope Happy had woven.

She arrived at the final knot just as he lunged away. She grabbed the end of the rope and hung on. Happy reached the hedge and slipped through, towing his mistress after him. Bayley found herself entangled in the hedge, and had just about made up her mind to let the darn fool go when somebody said, "Can I help you?"

Flat on her stomach, Bayley peered into the next yard.

The boy next door had cornered Happy and was addressing her, ignoring the indignity of her position. Now, to make her look even sillier, Happy darted back to kiss her again and thank her.

Bayley scrambled up. Her green dress was a mess. She was on the far side of the hedge now, and saw that a big yellow cat was backed against the Sudaks' porch, hissing with rage. "Happy won't hurt your cat," she said. "Actually, he loves everybody. He can't get it through his thick head that everybody doesn't love him back. He's kind of stupid that way."

"Is that your philosophy also?" the boy inquired.

Bayley was getting a good look at him. He was a tall drink of water, as Chip had described him, and his dark eyes were too big for his thin face. He had rather a fragile look. Bayley thought her mother would say he had shot up too fast to his six feet. His voice was low, and he had an Oxford accent, which was a real contrast to the flat tones Bayley was used to.

"It's a good philosophy," the boy went on. "It's too bad that it doesn't work. Perhaps he learned it from you?"

Then, embarrassed, he leaned over to pet the dog. "I'm sorry, that was a very personal remark. I am Bruno Sudak. I should have introduced myself before I started discussing your dog's private convictions."

"I'm Bayley Hughes."

He straightened up and started to click his heels, then relaxed. "I'm delighted to meet you, Miss Hughes."

44

"You have a sister," Bayley stated. "You're twins. Maybe my brother Chip told you that Benjy and I are twins, too. And the funny thing is that Chip says you and your sister will be juniors with us in school next fall."

"That is so." The nicest, warmest smile lit the boy's face. When he smiled, you forgot how scrawny he was, and how badly dressed in a frayed sport shirt of hideous color and design.

"Your father's something," Bayley went on, "but I forget what."

"My father is a chemist."

"Well, there's more to it than that, but I forget what it is." Bayley took the bull by the horns. "I'd love to meet your sister."

He turned towards his house, then hesitated. "Saja would like to meet you, too, but she is busy, I think. And Saja is timid with strangers. I'm the bold one of the family."

Astonished, Bayley protested, "We're not strangers. We're next-door neighbors. My mother's away, taking care of her aunt who broke her hip, but if she were here she'd have been knocking on your door long before this, to tell your mother 'welcome.' "

Now it was Bruno's turn to look startled. "Your mother would have come to knock on our door? What a pleasant custom." He added, under his breath, "What a beautiful custom."

"For Pete's sake!" Bayley exclaimed. "What did you expect? How about the Welcome Wagon? Didn't it come? It's supposed to, when new people move to town. They bring free presents, all kinds of stuff, and if you have problems about getting settled they help you. I thought I saw the Welcome Wagon in this street one day. I supposed it came here."

He said slowly, "It did. At least, the wagon sounds like what my mother described. It had signs on it, and someone came to the door. My father and sister and I were at the university at the time. I'm afraid she wouldn't unlock the door. She didn't understand."

"Is that your mother now?" A woman in black was hovering at the kitchen window. Bayley gave a friendly wave. The curtain dropped.

Bruno said abruptly, "I'm sorry, I must go in." Happy was pawing at his legs, and the boy sank to his knees to hug the warm, wriggling hound for a wordless moment. Then he started away.

Bayley called after him, "Will I see you again? And I want to meet your sister."

He turned. "Thank you. Thank you very much."

"Thank you for what?" Bayley asked.

"I think it's 'Thank you for being our neighbor,'" Bruno Sudak said slowly.

Bayley saw that his mother met him at the door and actually seemed to reach out and pull him inside, as though she was rescuing her son. Rescuing him from what? Bayley wondered. She wasn't angry, but she was really confused. Do I look like such a terrible person that

46

Mrs. Sudak is afraid to have her son associate with me? she wondered.

Her own father was calling from an upstairs window, "Bayley, come in. I have a plan."

Still musing over the encounter, Bayley ushered Happy into the house and absent-mindedly tossed him a few dog biscuits. Finally, she dismissed Bruno Sudak from her mind, concluding, He's weird, and the rest of his family seems even weirder. But he's got a lovely smile, and I hope I see him again.

She met her father on the stairs. "I've thought of something I'd like to do," he announced, "and I hope you want to do it with me."

"What, Dad?"

"Let's go and visit that game farm we read about, the one where they have the deer."

"But Dad, that's about fifty miles away."

"Maybe so, but it's only two o'clock. We'd have a chance to see the animals, and then I'd take you somewhere for supper."

She threw her arms around him. "Dad, it's a super idea. Do you really want to do it, though, or are you just afraid I'm bored?"

"No," he said, "I'm only consulting my own selfish pleasure."

"I never knew you to have any burning interest in deer before," she said happily. "You surprise me. I'll write a note for the boys and be ready in two shakes."

47

They were traveling along the highway when he elaborated on the reason for this sudden venture. "I decided we ought to improve this shining afternoon," he said. "If I'd thought of it earlier, we'd have kept Chip home to go with us. But it's been a long time, daughter, since you and I went anywhere alone.

"Besides," he added, "I was thinking, and I didn't like what I was thinking about. Oh, maybe I snored a bit, but I was thinking, all right!"

"What about?"

"Nothing of world-shaking importance. Actually, it's a minor office problem. I bring them home sometimes, to try them out on your mother, and now that she's away I guess you're next best as a listener."

He went on to explain. He pointed out how he had hesitated about transferring to Fenfield, although the change meant a promotion. He had liked the Brentford job, he said, because it meant traveling around, supervising gasoline storage installations and spot-checking. Here in Fenfield, he was tied to a desk. This was a larger division, and he had more men under him.

"The advantages outweigh the disadvantages," he mused, "the chief one being the university. After we drag you four young-uns up to the proper age, then your ma and I have to see that you're educated. We couldn't manage college for you all unless you live at home. After all, there will be a period of several years when we'll have two or even three in college at the same time."

"Dad, you said you had a problem at the office," Bayley reminded him.

"Yes," he said, "although it's not the type of thing anyone can help with, or even advise me on. It's a chap named Scott Aylsworth. He had every right to expect he'd step into my job, and he's disappointed that a man was brought in from outside. I've tried to establish a friendly relationship, but he won't reciprocate. He makes small snide remarks, not pointed enough so I can call him on them, but they get under my skin."

Indignantly, Bayley exclaimed, "Why, the horrid little man!"

"No, he's not a horrid man, just a frustrated one," her father said. "Well, it'll work out. As a matter of fact, having told somebody about it makes me feel better."

He went on, "I saw you talking with the boy next door. What about him? Did you like him?"

"Yes. I'd say, though, we've really got a weird set of neighbors, Dad. How about the father? Bruno says he's a chemist, but it seems to me I heard something more about him."

"There's considerably more about him than just being a chemist," Mr. Hughes said drily. "I asked a couple of questions downtown. It seems that our neighbor is *the* Dr. Sigmund Sudak, who shared a Nobel Prize recently with three other men in England, for some important discovery. It seems that the university has been angling for a long time to get him over here.

49

"It's queer, isn't it? Many of the world's truly important men rarely get into the papers, and the rest of us ignorant clods probably never even hear about them. Then one of them quietly moves next door to us."

"For heaven's sakes," Bayley said. "A Nobel Prize winner." She thought that over for a while, then asked, "Did you hear anything about his wife or daughter? I wonder why they're so scared. Mrs. Sudak wouldn't let the Welcome Wagon ladies in. And I haven't gotten a good look at the daughter."

"I have the answer to that, too," her father said. "The wife's name is Jadwega. Mrs. Sudak was a student when the last war began, and she spent years in concentration camps under the Nazis. After the war she was shut up again by the Russians in another camp, and it was there she met her husband. They managed somehow to get out, but for several more years they lived in refugee camps set up by the Allies, and their children were born in one. Finally, when Dr. Sudak's identity was cleared up, the family was taken to England, where they've lived until now.

"Dr. Sudak is chairman of the chemistry department at the university, but he's also heading up some hush-hush project for the government. I guess he's one of the brainiest men in the world. The English thought so, anyway. The Russians and the Germans were too stupid to realize the caliber of the man they were holding."

"But why is his wife so frightened?" Bayley persisted.

"I don't know. However, I can guess, daughter, that

anything you can do in the way of being neighborly would be very worthwhile. I wish your mother was home. She has a marvelous knack for making friends. Why don't you try and see what you can do?"

They arrived at the game farm. A fine store fronted on the highway, its show windows filled with mink coats. Bayley paused to look at them, wondering, Will I ever own a real mink coat?

They passed through a stile into the wild-animal exhibit, and started along a grassy aisle between cages. An automatic machine dispensed bags of animal food, and Mr. Hughes fed nickels into it until Bayley's hands were full. She began feeding the lively, humorous-looking raccoons which crowded to the wire.

Suddenly, she realized that she was surrounded. A buck and four does, wandering loose through the crowd, had singled her out. She fed them, but they became really insistent. One doe stood on its hind legs, its slim front feet on her shoulders. Bayley gently tried to push the delicate creature away. People had gathered around, laughing, and a man snapped a picture of her. "Get more food, quick, Dad!" Bayley cried.

The photographer had a camera which developed pictures immediately. He sold Mr. Hughes the shot of Bayley for twenty-five cents. "It's a nice souvenir of your visit," he said.

Bayley and her father wandered on and arrived at the mink cage. It was arranged like a small amusement area. The minks' chief delight seemed to be the slide, which

51

ended in a pool of water. The small, elegant creatures raced to the top and slid joyously down, landing splashing in the pool.

It was fascinating to watch, but Bayley grew silent and thoughtful. Finally, she turned away. "Have you seen enough?" her father asked.

"I guess so. Let's go."

The only exit from the animal area led through the store, where the fur coats were displayed. A salesman came forward. "How do you do, sir. Could I interest you in something for your daughter?" He put one of the coats around Bayley's shoulders.

She wriggled out of it. "No, thank you," she said, and marched out of the store.

Her father looked at her curiously. "Is anything wrong, daughter?"

"No," she said. "It was just that I hated the feel of that coat, after seeing the minks in their cage having such a lovely time. I guess that if I ever wanted a mink coat, I've changed my mind."

"I wasn't exactly planning on buying you one," he assured her. Then they both laughed. He went on, "It's seven o'clock. We'd better think about supper."

He stopped at a restaurant that specialized in pizza, one of Bayley's favorite foods.

It was late when they turned into their own drive. "Oh, no, not on Sunday!" Mr. Hughes exclaimed. "Our poor neighbors!"

From the cellar wafted the unmistakable racket of the

amateur jazz combo. Bayley knew one sure, quick way to end this disturbance. She ran into the house and called down the cellar stairs, "Chip, if you and your friends will come I'll make you a batch of fudge."

The racket stopped in the middle of a phrase.

She watched the late news with her father. The boys were quietly making themselves ill over a plate of fudge. "You're quite a manager," Mr. Hughes said admiringly. "Your mother couldn't have handled it better."

"Dad, it's been a super day. Thanks for everything."

V

BAYLEY WROTE her mother about the Sunday outing. She was feeling conversational anyway.

"Darling Mother," she wrote. "Dad and I felt badly we couldn't see you yesterday, and I guess Dad was worried about Aunt Bayley, and missed you, too, so he took me on an expedition. We went to a game farm. I'm enclosing a snapshot. The deer were darling, they had the softest lips, they ate out of our hands.

"But the thing that absolutely threw me was a cageful of mink. Mother, they were just sweet. When we left we had to go through a store full of fur coats, and a man tried to sell Dad one, and I decided I never want to own one. Never. Not after seeing those sweet little animals.

"I guess you'll think I'm nuts the way I run on, but I just feel like talking. Dad's a terribly nice guy, did you know that? I suppose you do, you married him. I suggested he could teach me how to play cribbage. I thought I could take your place at it until you get back.

"You'll want to know about the boys. They're fine.

Tom spends all his evenings with Beth. Mother, do you really think she's the right girl for him? I am just not sure. I told him to invite her for dinner here, and he turned a pale green.

"Benjy's car is about in the same state as when you left. Now it's the carburetor, but with that car if it isn't one thing it's another.

"Chip isn't home much, but I'm not worried, he is not a juvenile delinquent, I don't want you to be concerned about that. His pleasures are innocent and normally boyish I am sure. You would be slightly appalled by his latest. He has gotten Tim Healy and Charlie to join him in a jazz combo, but so far I have handled the problem very well. I have shut them in the cellar, and when I see that Dad is about to blow his stack, I feed them to make them stop playing. I have a strong feeling, however, that this project will soon die a natural death. The sessions grow shorter and shorter. I guess it is hard for boys that age to sit still for long at a time.

"I'll tell you about our new neighbors in my next, they will need a letter all to themselves.

"I could write a whole letter full of my small domestic problems. I doubt I will ever truly get the hang of this housekeeping. I think I'll marry a rich man. I'd do better as an old man's darling than I would living in a cottage by a waterfall and trying to keep up with this rat race.

"I was thinking, Mother, that if you have any free moments you might devote them to one of my personal problems. I actually looked at myself in the mirror the

55

other day and eeek! I am skinnier than ever. For instance, my friend Jean is getting a real bosom, which she calls 'bo-soom.' But me? Nothing. In front I look about ten years old.

"My date situation is not good. Do you remember how before you went away we talked about doing something to me and my clothes? We didn't get very far along on that project. You're such a darn good-looking female, I wish I'd listened to you when you tried to lecture to me about the grooming bit.

"Mother, Aunt Bayley's going to be all right, isn't she? I mean, we always think she's indestructible. I mean, nothing can happen to Aunt Bayley.

"Mother, if I write any more I'm going to get homesick for you, so will close now.

Your ever lovin',
Bayley."

She was pleased she had had to go to the dictionary only twice, for the spelling of "delinquent" and "indestructible." She stamped the letter and walked to the corner to mail it. She rather dawdled as she passed the house next door, hoping to get a glimpse of the mysterious Sudaks. Particularly, she hoped to see the father.

Only that morning, when Jean called for their usual chat over the phone, Bayley had told her, awed, "Dr. Sudak won a Nobel Prize."

"Bully for him," Jean had said.

Since Jean was the only girl friend Bayley had acquired so far in Fenfield, she let this go. However, it did make

56

her long for the friends she had grown up with in Brentford who might have been more impressed.

She inquired after Jean's permanent. Then they talked about boys for a while, and made a date to go to a movie that evening. Jean worked that around to getting herself invited to the Hughes house for dinner, at which time she could reasonably expect Benjy to be present.

When you moved to a new town, you were lucky to pick up any friends right away. Jean was all right, even if she was in the toils of a consuming passion for Bayley's twin.

Dr. Sudak did not conveniently emerge from his front door as Bayley passed. Of course, they weren't going to have any great bond, she sensibly realized. Her one year in high-school chemistry wasn't going to enable her to converse on the high scientific plane Dr. Sudak operated on. But she had it in mind at least to say, "Oh, Dr. Sudak, all of us are immensely thrilled that you have moved into our midst."

She turned into her own yard, and met Chip in the act of toting the rubbish cans to the curb. No one had asked him to, or even reminded him that today was rubbish-collection day. This was so unaccountably thoughtful of tow-headed Chip that Bayley threw her arms around him. "Hey, leggo!" Chip yelled, overcome with horror at being embraced in public by a sister.

The Sudak girl was in her back yard, hanging clothes. This was the first time Bayley had really gotten a good look at her. She and her brother had the same too tall, too narrow frame, the same enormous eyes. The girl's hair must have been extremely long, for it was wound around her head in a coronet, and that, Bayley guessed, meant an awful lot of hair.

Bayley took all this in at a glance. At the same time, she noticed that the laundry Saja was pinning to the line had a bad case of tattle-tale gray.

In Brentford, the Hughes family had charged back and forth through neighbors' yards as though they were public property. Now Bayley saw no reason to stand on ceremony. She slipped through the hedge, and as the startled girl swung around Bayley stuck out her hand. Saja, confused, took it. "I'm Bayley Hughes. I guess maybe your brother told you we had a nice talk one day. I'm glad to meet you, Saja."

The girl's blush spread upward to her hair. "Thank you very much," she stammered.

"There's nothing to thank me for," Bayley said. "I just thought it was high time I came over to say 'Hello.' Here, let me help you." She began taking towels out of the basket, pinning them on the line. They seemed somewhat ragged.

Saja tried to stop her. "No, you mustn't. Thank you very much, but I will do it."

Together, they put on the last pins. Bayley tried to make conversation, about the nice yards both houses had, about school next fall. Saja didn't think to ask her to sit down on a bench nearby.

Suddenly Saja broke in. "I'm sorry, Miss Hughes—

58

Bayley. I must go in. There is a great deal of washing left to do."

"Don't you have a machine?"

"A washing machine? No."

Bayley trotted out her most winning smile. "We've got an automatic and luckily it was fixed this morning. Let's put your clothes in our machine, and we can have a nice visit while they're getting washed."

Saja tried every excuse to avoid this, but to no avail. Bayley was intent on doing a good deed; she had really gotten her teeth into it, and refused to take Saja's refusal.

Saja finally gave in and disappeared into the house. Bayley waited outside, hearing her arguing with her mother in rapid Polish. Finally she emerged, carrying a basketful of laundry. Bayley seized it and Saja, still protesting, trailed after her to the Hughes cellar.

Efficiently, Bayley loaded the machine. She was getting quite good at this laundry business; her men went through clean clothes so fast that washing was a daily chore. She added a cup of bleach, for the sheets and pillow cases badly needed whitening.

She had some qualms. Maybe she was acting rather pushy and arrogant. Saja will forgive me, though, when she sees how nicely the things come out, Bayley told herself.

She led the way upstairs, made lemonade and piled cookies on a plate and carried the tray out to the back yard. She fussily seated Saja in the most comfortable chair. "There!" Bayley exclaimed with satisfaction.

59

However, making conversation didn't get any easier. Bayley realized that Bruno was a regular chatterbox compared to his sister. Saja perched tensely, watching her own house. Bayley doggedly continued to ask questions, and managed to find out that the twins had been born in a refugee camp in Germany, that their schooling had been sketchy until they went to live in London, that Saja spoke German, French, English, and Polish. Yes, Saja liked the United States, what little she had seen.

Her face softened when Bayley said, "I bet you're awfully proud of your father."

Saja's smile was almost radiant. "Yes."

"He must be smart. I mean," Bayley said, "he must be what you'd have to call brilliant, to win a Nobel Prize and all."

"Yes," Saja said, weighing her words carefully as she did in everything she said, "he is brilliant, but he is a very kind father, too."

"And brave," Bayley said. "I guess he and your mother were both brave to survive the war and all."

"Yes. My mother—" Saja stopped.

Bayley prompted her. "You were speaking about your mother."

"I was going to say that I hope the women in this town will not misjudge her. She has had a very hard life, and she has been ill. She is not well yet." Again Bayley waited, but Saja did not go on.

Finally, they went down-cellar, took the laundry out

of the machine, and piled it in the basket. "It looks so white!" Saja marveled.

"That's just good old American know-how," Bayley said airily. She insisted on helping to hang the wash on the Sudaks' line, and was pleased to see how bright it looked, billowing in the wind.

Saja took her hand when she started to leave. "I must seem odd to you," she stammered. "I think it is because our parents have brought us up in the old-country ways. We don't know yet how to meet Americans. Bayley, will you be patient with us? Bruno and I want to be friends, too, but we have to learn how."

In quite an exalted mood, Bayley marched home. Benjy was in the kitchen. The bass fiddle and the trumpet were making a wobbly duet in the cellar. Bayley heard Chip stamping, "One, two."

Benjy was pouring himself a Coke. "Oh, dear," Bayley exclaimed, "I only left the house a minute ago, and they sneaked in. Here I've put in an afternoon trying to convince Saja Sudak that we're a normal, average family, and now she'll think she's moved next door to an offbeat outfit."

"As far as that goes," her twin said, "I understand that Mrs. Sudak acts sort of peculiar. Maybe she'll feel right at home."

"That's a silly thing to say!" Bayley flared up. She went on to tell all she had learned about the new neighbors.

61

Benjy conceded that what he knew he had heard second-hand. Bayley and Benjy, despite the fact that they sometimes quarreled bitterly, and between quarrels kept up a sniping warfare, usually reacted identically to new situations. Now Benjy said agreeably, "I'll take your word for it, they're okay, and I'll see what I can do about getting acquainted with this Bruno character."

"It'll be a lot easier for them when they start school if they know two people in the class," Bayley pointed out. "Saja said they had been raised in the old-country ways, and that's all right, I guess, but maybe we can graft on some new-country ways. Then they won't stick out like a couple of sore thumbs."

VI

THERE WAS NO DOUBT of it: Bayley was beginning to get the hang of what she called "the home-making bit." She saw that it didn't have to be the rat race it had seemed when her mother first went away. When she was a child, she had strongly resisted learning what the word "routine" meant. Now routine was becoming her way of life.

The first thing in the morning, she leaped out of bed, threw cold water on her face, and dashed downstairs. By feats of magic, she slapped three breakfasts on the table simultaneously: bacon and eggs and toast for Tom and her father, dry cereal and milk for Benjy. Her youngest brother had such an erratic schedule that she let him forage for himself.

After the men departed, the house belonged to her. Chip was around, but he had projects in the yard or in the garage, or was away doing odd lawn jobs in order to earn money. His platoons of friends hung around while he did whatever it was.

Chip was like a magnet, the way he attracted like-minded friends. Or "fiends," as Benjy pointed out, "if you just drop the 'R.' " What Chip called his jazz combo was a real source of anguish to his brother. Bayley liked good jazz, but Benjy was the one with a really sensitive ear for it. He claimed that if the three so-called musicians practiced for a thousand years they would never produce anything except total chaos. Bayley, too, thought that Chip could have waited until the family made some sort of place for itself in the quiet community, before he proceeded to wreck the peace.

However, in the mornings Chip, Tim, good old Charlie, and the other hangers-on were usually away carrying on their money-making enterprises. Bayley had the big house to herself.

She raced through the dishes, then dashed through the bed-making. She learned that a few fast flourishes with a dust mop made the upstairs look neat. Maybe the mop only sent dust kittens scurrying under the bureaus, but she considered that "Out of sight, out of mind" was a sensible motto for any housekeeper.

She dealt with her brothers' clutter by tossing it into their closets. When they complained, she loftily reminded them, "People ought to take better care of their possessions and not leave them around," to which they had no answer.

Descending to the first floor again, Bayley watered the violets, fed Happy, dragged him out and tied him on his rope, gave the furniture a lick and a promise with the duster, and then flopped in a chair to telephone Jean.

The talk ranged over boys, clothes, what they planned to do with their lives, and back to boys. After the laundromat episode, Jerry had made himself scarce. Thus, Bayley had little to contribute to the talk about boys, but Jean had a real thing about Benjy. Since Jean was Bayley's only real female friend, Bayley was trying to encourage this affair. Benjy's only response so far had been a surly "Lay off me."

Bayley felt it would be smart to enlarge this narrow circle of girl friends. She told Jean about her encounter with Saja and assured Jean, "You'll like her." In her heart, however, she wasn't at all sure the two girls would get along.

She and Jean exchanged what news there was, and usually this consumed an hour. Bayley's routine next took her to the kitchen, where she surveyed the food situation. This varied from bad to hopeless. Her men went through the larder like locusts, consuming everything in their path.

Bayley listed the needed items. After this she pushed the cart to the supermarket. This was one task she really enjoyed. The store contained solutions to many of her problems.

She discovered the charms of the frozen-food department, and planning meals ceased to be a nightmare. At first, when she served the small prepared pies, her family rejoiced. The way they gobbled them up wasn't too flattering, in contrast to the way they picked at the dinners she spent hours cooking. However, Bayley was developing a thicker skin that was impervious to their sarcasm. In rapid succession she tried out turkey pies, meat pies, tuna-fish pies.

65

About the time the men began to turn sullen at the sight of frozen pies, Bayley discovered frozen dinners. Again, her family's enthusiasm was kindled afresh. But when, for the third night in a row, Tom found himself confronted by an aluminum tray holding dollops of mashed potatoes, peas, and meat, he demanded, "What's happened to the old-fashioned art of cooking?"

"These dinners are balanced, nutritious, and delicious," Bayley informed him.

"But scanty."

"The American people eat too much."

"Not these Americans. We're rapidly joining the ranks of the chronically underfed," Tom rejoined.

"You can fill up on bread," Bayley advised. "Then you can give a thought to the people in India and China and elsewhere who are getting along on nine hundred calories a day, and you'll realize how lucky you are."

"All I can say is, I hope Mother gets home before we turn into walking skeletons," Benjy finished grimly.

Their mother was faithful about writing. Finally, a letter came to let them know that Aunt Bayley was well enough to leave the hospital. On the Sunday after she had been settled in her own apartment, the family drove over to see her.

Bayley was assailed by homesickness as her father drove through the familiar streets of Brentford. Maybe it lacked a university and the cultural advantages of Fenfield, but it still seemed like home.

They took the elevator to Aunt Bayley's three-room

apartment. After hugging their mother thoroughly, they filed into the bedroom.

Bayley's heart sank. Her aunt looked very frail. However, even if she was confined to her bed, Aunt Bayley showed that her spirit had suffered no damage. Her blue eyes were as alert and bright as ever. "Phew!" she said. "Ben, put out that terrible cigar! Well, dears, here I am flat on my back, and isn't this a pretty kettle of fish? I bet it's the first time any of you ever came to see me and found me dawdling in bed."

"She's getting cantankerous," Mrs. Hughes informed them. "She's bound and determined she's going to teach next September."

Aunt Bayley had taught fourth grade in the Brentford schools all her life, and had only a year to go before retirement.

"She'll do it, too," Tom said, studying his aunt with pride.

"I know she will," his mother agreed.

"What's new?" Aunt Bayley demanded. "Let's not talk about me. Bayley, how do you like keeping house?"

"Ugh," Bayley said.

"Your men-folks don't look as though they're exactly withering away. But I'm sending your ma back with you, to stay a week. I've got friends, other teachers living in this building. They'll look after me."

"No," Mr. Hughes said. "We loaned Elizabeth to you until you get on your feet, Aunt Bayley."

At first, Bayley's heart had lifted at the suggestion that

her mother might come home. Then it sank. She thought about the house and the horrible condition it really was in. Her men wouldn't give her away, because they actually didn't see the dust kittens, the disorder, the lack of care. But her mother's sharp eyes would, and although she wouldn't say anything, she would be disappointed.

"That's right," Bayley agreed. "You need Mother more than we do."

Her aunt's thin hand found Elizabeth's and clung to it. The bond between them was warm and close. "I can't say I don't enjoy the loan of your mother," she said.

"But everything's all right at home?" Mrs. Hughes asked.

When the boys loudly reassured her, Bayley thought, They really are a pretty loyal lot.

Chip, rather surprised to hear the others lying so handily, said, "Yeah, Mom, but you ought to speak to Bay about those tin frozen dinners. We're starved!" Benjy gave him a punch to shut him up.

"Your ma has fixed you a genteel collation in the other room," Aunt Bayley said. "Why don't you men go and eat, and leave Bayley to talk to me?"

Alone with her aunt, Bayley took the thin hand, which felt paper cool. "Do you really intend to teach next year?" she asked.

"I certainly do. I'll retire at seventy and not a day before. I'll finish my stint and collect a gold watch for it," Aunt Bayley said briskly. "Now let's talk about you, child. Are you having a good summer?"

"Oh, lovely!"

"You don't have to put on act with me."

"Yes, I guess I'm having a good summer."

"What are you doing that's worthwhile?"

That caught Bayley up short. This relative had a devastating way of cutting to the heart of any subject. "I'm keeping the house going. You said yourself I'm taking good care of the boys," she stammered.

"That's not what I mean, child. Running a house is only a means to an end. Are you reading some good books? Are you getting over your tomboy ways? Are you making any interesting friends?"

Bayley tried to laugh off the questions. "For heaven's sakes, Aunt Bayley, you're awfully nosy!"

The old lady's eyes softened. "I know I am. And yet a whole summer is a big bite out of a girl's growing-up time. Lying in the hospital in that doggoned cast, I thought about you a lot. Sometimes I wonder if you ever stop to think how the days are running away from you. They do, you know; they run away from all of us. Then one day we wake up, as I have, finding myself trapped in bed this way, and we ask, 'Where is it all gone?' And our lives are almost over, as though the wind picked up the years and whisked them away."

She took Bayley's hand and smoothed it. "Don't pay me any mind," she said softly. "I get to feeling sorry for myself because you had to move away and I'm missing watching you grow up. Now, tell me about the family that moved next door to you. Your letters made them sound interesting."

Bayley gave her what she had to tell. She had to admit

that, after the day she had lured Saja over for a visit, she had made little progress. "Maybe they don't really want to be friends," she concluded. "I was too pushy that day, forcing myself on Saja."

"I doubt that's the case," her aunt said. "I've thought about their background, and all they've been through. I've thought about the father, who must be a really brilliant man, the mother who is so frightened, the two children who have grown up in that atmosphere and are trying to find their way in a new country. I'd say, Bayley, you'll have to make even more of an effort.

"We spoke about making this a memorable summer," she concluded. "It would be quite a feather in your cap, darling, if you succeeded in making the Sudaks glad they had come to Fenfield to live."

Mrs. Hughes came in then with a tray for the invalid, and Bayley fed her aunt. All through the process, although she was obviously enjoying the attention, Aunt Bayley fussed and snorted.

Mr. Hughes spoke about that on the way back to Fenfield. "She hasn't changed an iota," he said with satisfaction. "Your mother has done a remarkable job. Your aunt's spirit hasn't been impaired in the slightest."

"Do you really thinks she looks all right, Dad?" Benjy asked.

"Yes. And now we know that when she gets to be a hundred she'll still be battling."

Tom, who was driving the car, laughed. "Do you remember when all of us in turn had Aunt Bayley for a teacher in the fourth grade?" he reminded the others. "Remember how much rougher she was on us than on anybody else? I bet that every kid who had Aunt Bay in the fourth grade, and survived it, found he'd been picked up by his collar and thoroughly shaken up. That year we spent in her room set us on the path we were to follow forever after.

"She was strict; she was always fair; and I think she absolutely adored every kid, good or bad. I bet each one of us, looking back, sees that year as the turning point when we began to have a respect for education."

"Yes," Benjy said, "I remember I could never get it straight in spelling, whether 'I' came before 'E' or the other way around. I'll never forget the day she decided I wasn't going to make that mistake again. She made me write 'I before E except after C' five hundred times, in a notebook. Then she started chanting, and the whole class joined in, 'I before E, except after C,' and she stood in the aisle by my desk, whacking me over the head with the notebook.

"After that, whenever I came to a word with those letters in it, I never made a mistake. My head always started ringing!"

They all had reminiscences of Aunt Bayley as a teacher. Talking about her carried them the rest of the way home.

That night, when she was getting ready for bed, Bayley thought over the day. Aunt Bayley had brightened their spirits. "She's like a shot in the arm" was the way Benjy had put it. But the dear, lovable thing about this remarkable relative was the way her mind was always occupied with the problems of others, never with her own. She had been thinking about her namesake through those long days in the hospital, not hoping that Bayley was having a fun kind of summer, but truly concerned that she was making the summer count for something.

Bayley looked from her window across to the Sudak house. She could see right into the dining-room window, where the twins were reading at a big round table, the old-fashioned glass chandelier lighting the red tablecloth. Mrs. Sudak was sewing. Bayley guessed that the professor was in his workshop in the cellar, because there was a light down there.

"I'll make a real effort to be a good neighbor," Bayley decided. "I won't put it off. It'll be interesting anyway, and at least I can write Aunt Bayley that I'm really trying."

VII

"SAY, NUISANCE, how about riding over to Eastbrook with me this morning?" Tom suggested one day at breakfast. "I have to take a piece of machinery to the foundry to be repaired."

Bayley was flattered. However, she was suspicious, because it had been a long time since Tom had invited her anywhere. "I'd like to go, but what about Beth?"

"She has classes," Tom told her. "She's trying to get a couple of education credits this summer, at the university."

"I thought so," Bayley said. It was only the fact that his girl was otherwise occupied that reminded him he might enjoy his sister's company.

Bayley didn't let this spoil her pleasure. She rode to the factory with Tom, then waited in the truck while the heavy machine was loaded. Soon, they were driving along the highway to Eastbrook, twenty miles away. "I'm glad you asked me to come," she said.

"Glad to have you aboard."

"It was too bad Beth couldn't come," Bayley added politely.

At that, Tom's face softened. Any mention of his beloved had this effect on him.

"She's awfully smart," Bayley went on, leaning over backward to be generous.

"Yes, she gives me a real inferiority complex. She runs circles around me when it comes to getting good grades."

"Oh, well," Bayley consoled him, "girls are naturally smarter than boys. Look at Benjy and me. He really sweats and strains over the easiest courses. But they say that after a while boys catch up."

Tom didn't exactly view this as comfort. It reminded him of areas where boys usually excelled. "How's your tennis, Toots?"

"I never get a chance to practice. I haven't played since you and I went to the college courts before school closed."

"We'll have to get in some tennis soon."

"When?" Bayley asked, hoping to pin him down.

He slid out of that. "Some night after work, maybe, when I'm not tied up. Okay?"

"Okay."

"I imagine you're pretty well dated up yourself," he mentioned.

"I wouldn't say that," she said frankly. "I don't know why I don't make friends as easily as Chip, for instance. I want to, it isn't that. But I haven't had one honest-to-gosh date this summer, if I don't count the time Jerry Flint took me and our dirty clothes to the laundromat. He only did that out of the kindness of his heart."

"You'll meet some kids you like," Tom said easily.

Today, for the first time in a long time, Bayley had this brother to herself, a captive audience so to speak, and she decided she might as well profit from the occasion. "Don't put me off, Tom," she said. "What's wrong with me? Don't give me the obvious reasons, because I know them. I'm too scrawny and too muscular, and maybe I've spent too much time playing sports with you boys, so I never developed those alluring curves girls are supposed to have. But it's more than that. I really want an answer. Why do I put boys off?"

He said, "Are you sure you don't just want a buttering-up?"

"No, I really want to know. Maybe it's something even my best friends won't tell me, like I use the wrong soap or something. So just forget you're my best friend."

He chuckled. "You use the right soap, I guess." He paused before going on. "Maybe it's because you're too fast on the uptake, Bay. Or maybe you're kind of prickly. Boys don't really like girls who are too soft and mushy, but you make me think of a prickly pear. You're nice on the inside; all of us in the family know that. But you're unpredictable. You have spells of being shy and retiring, and then you suddenly get really pushy. Not exactly pushy—I don't mean that—but too direct.

"Now take your looks," Tom went on, warming to the job of setting his sister straight. "Just because you and Benjy are twins doesn't mean you have to have your hair cut like his. On Benjy a brush looks all right, but it doesn't do a thing for you. And what do you do to your hair? One quick pass in the morning with a comb—I bet that's all the attention it gets.

"Then take the matter of lipstick. If you're going to wear it, you ought to find out where your mouth is. Your lipstick looks as though you put it on in a dark closet. Then, take your clothes. You look great in dungarees or Bermudas, but you never look comfortable in dresses.

"Another thing, when are you going to stop biting your nails? You're a big girl now."

"I guess now I know pretty well what's wrong with me," Bayley laughed shakily. "You think if I put those things right, I'd do better? Jean's after me, too, about them. She wants to give me a permanent and show me how to do my nails."

"How could you reach the ripe old age of sixteen and not know those things?" Tom asked. "How come Ma never taught you?"

"Don't blame her, because she tried. She just couldn't pin me down long enough," Bayley said. "But this business of being pushy, that's kind of got me. The other day, Aunt Bayley told me I ought to cultivate the new people next door. You know, welcome them to the community and all that. I want to, but I don't know how to go about it. One day, I practically hauled Saja over to our house by the hair of her head, and grabbed her laundry away from her to show her how much better our machine could do it. She seemed really grateful, but ever since, when she sees me outdoors, she kind of scuttles off. Bruno, her brother, was friendly, too, when I talked to him. But he keeps to his own side of the hedge and calls, 'Good morning.' "

"Have you made any more efforts?"

"No, because I don't want to make any more mistakes."

"What would Mother do, if she were home?" Tom asked.

"I don't know."

"Well, I remember what she used to do in Brentford when new people moved to our street. She'd bake them something as a welcoming present, and dress up and go and call. Then she'd ask them to come to tea at our house. Lots of times I remember coming home from school and finding mother entertaining ladies at tea."

"I think you've got something there," Bayley said slowly. "What'll I bake them?"

"If you knew how to make a cake, that would be okay, but you don't," Tom said frankly.

"What if I bought a nice cake?"

"No, that wouldn't do. It has to show a friendly effort."

"I know! At the store they have a shelf of cake mixes. I've been thinking of trying them."

Tom asked, "Why didn't you ever take home ec? If anybody ever needed it, it's you."

"I couldn't fit it in because I'm taking the college-prep course," Bayley explained. "Jean takes it. Maybe she'll make me a cake."

"I'll tell you what," Tom suggested. "Why don't you try one of those mixes for dinner some time? Try it out on the dog, so to speak, your ever-lovin' family being the dog. If it comes out all right, then you can do it for the Sudaks. But don't try it on them first. You could set international relations back about fifty years!"

For the rest of the ride, they kept off personalities. None of Tom's criticisms had really hurt Bayley, however. After all, she had asked for it, and Tom had only been trying to help. Also, she recognized in Tom the superiority of the male who has found his soulmate. Naturally, a mere sister suffered in comparison with such a peerless creature as his Beth.

When they arrived home, Bayley rushed right off to the supermarket. She spent so much time poring over the array of cake mixes that Benjy joined her. "This isn't a library," he said. "How come you're doing your reading here?"

"I'm going to make some cakes."

"Oh, no!"

"Oh, yes!" Bayley assured him.

Benjy's hours were irregular, and it happened he had that afternoon free. It also happened that Jean went to the store to shop for her mother and found Benjy absent. Naturally, she dropped in at the Hughes house to see how Bayley was getting on. So Bayley had quite an audience in the kitchen.

Jean wanted to take over the job, but Bayley clung to her boxes, firmly pushing her away. "At least, you'll let me make the frosting," Jean suggested.

"No, but you can show me how."

Jean, with her slightly pug nose and shining hair, was

an attractive girl, and, furthermore, she had a dry humor which Bayley wouldn't have expected to find in a girl who was so boy-crazy. Anyway, Benjy found the company congenial. While Bayley was earnestly blending and mixing, Jean whipped up a pan of penuche for him, and that wasn't exactly calculated to alienate his affections. In fact, Benjy was regarding Jean with a new light in his eyes, and Bayley was glad to see it. At least, this afternoon was accomplishing that much.

It accomplished more—it resulted in two impressive cakes. Jean helped make a rich chocolate frosting for the white cake, a brown-sugar icing for the yellow. Happy, who got the bowls to lick, pronounced them equally good.

Bayley chopped nuts and liberally sprinkled the tops. "Now we have to decide which one goes to the Sudaks," she said.

"Do they get the best one?" Benjy demanded.

"Of course, and we'll cut the other to make sure it's all right."

"It'll be all right," Jean promised. "Those mixes are practically foolproof."

"Then you can cut the brown sugar one. I'm going up to dress."

"Don't worry," Jean assured her. "I won't let Benjy lay one little pinky on the Sudaks' cake."

While Bayley was dressing, she could hear the two scuffling in the kitchen, and guessed that Benjy was threatening to take a knife to the other cake. She put on her most becoming cotton dress, wet her auburn hair and slicked it down, and used her lipstick carefully, remembering what Tom had said about putting it on without looking.

When she returned to the kitchen, both Benjy and Jean were flushed, and Bayley knew that relations between her brother and her best friend were improving by leaps and bounds.

Benjy's eyes widened when he saw her. "I didn't know this was a state visit!"

"How about the white gloves?" Jean asked.

"What white gloves?"

"My mother's so square, when she makes a call she does the whole bit, white gloves and calling cards."

"Honestly?" Bayley asked, troubled.

"I was just kidding," Jean told her. "You look okay. You look great."

VIII

CAREFULLY BALANCING her gift, Bayley walked up the Sudaks' path and rang the bell. Instinct told her that this type of formal call should be made at the front door.

She caught a glimpse of Jadwega Sudak's white face behind the glass. Then it vanished. There was a long wait, and she heard whispering inside. It was Bruno who opened the door.

A ghastly pause ensued. Bayley reddened and blurted, "I've come to call on your mother. Is she at home?"

Bruno didn't ask her in, but she sidled through the door anyway. "Yes, my mother is here," Bruno said in a low voice, "but she is not well enough to see anybody." His courtesy reasserted itself and he suggested, "Won't you sit down? I'll find Saja."

Bayley set the cake on the center table, took a leather chair, and surveyed the living room. It was far from tidy. The usual television set was missing, and also the curtains. The chairs were hard and slippery. The rug was worn and frayed. Books crowded the shelves on either side of the fireplace, and the overflow was piled higgledy-piggledy in every corner. They weren't ordinary books with bright jackets; they all seemed to be heavy, scientific-type tomes.

Saja came straight to Bayley and took her hand. "This is another instance of your kindness," she said.

"I brought you a cake," Bayley explained.

"That was very thoughtful."

"Oh, no, not at all," Bayley demurred.

"Is it the custom of your country?" inquired Saja.

"Yes, I guess so. If my mother weren't away taking care of my aunt, she'd have come the first week to call on your mother." Then Bayley took the bull by the horns. "I'd like to meet her," she said firmly.

Brother and sister exchanged glances, and Saja said, "I'm sorry. This is one of her poor days."

Unexpectedly, Bruno took charge. "This is the first cake we have had in this house since we came here," he said.

"Then I'm glad I'm the one who brought it," Bayley told him. The graceful little remark made the other two smile.

"We will go in the dining room and have coffee," Bruno announced. He held the door for his sister and Bayley, and then Saja left them to make the coffee.

Here again, books were piled everywhere. A box of stones occupied the center of the table, and this surprised Bayley. They seemed to be just ordinary rocks.

She smoothed the red tablecloth. "I look out of my window and see you here in the evenings," she confessed. "Oh, I don't mean to be snoopy! But you all look as though you're having a good time together." She laughed and added, "Now I suppose you'll pull down the shade. You didn't know you had a Peeping Tom."

Bruno was sitting with his back to the heavy drapes that shut off the hall. Bayley saw a white hand draw them aside, and she almost cried out when Mrs. Sudak's face appeared. The dark eyes were enormous and seemed full of terror.

Bruno followed Bayley's glance and got up quickly. Bayley heard them talking in rapid Polish in the dark hall. She guessed that Bruno was trying to draw his mother into the room. But when he came back, he made no reference to Mrs. Sudak.

Saja entered then, carrying a heavy tray, and her brother leaped up to clear the table for her. The coffee Saja poured was thick and strong. She set out plates and started to cut the cake. "You don't have to cut it now," Bayley protested. "You can save it for your supper."

"Oh, but it will be so pleasant for Papa when he comes to find us having a party," Saja said.

Bayley sipped her coffee. Saja must have seen that she made a small grimace, for she said, "I forgot. Of course, you like cream in it. I'm sorry we have no cream, but we have milk."

When she returned from the kitchen she was carrying a small pitcher of milk. She had just set it down, when Mrs. Sudak darted into the room. She seized the pitcher from Bayley's hand, and in a rush of Polish, waving and gesticulating, scolded her daughter.

Saja kissed her mother and took the milk from her, and

83

Mrs. Sudak disappeared. This time when Saja came back from the kitchen, the milk was in a silver pitcher. "My mother was afraid you would be offended because I offered it to you in such a poor china container," she explained.

Bayley realized then that Mrs. Sudak was watching their every move. "I do wish she would come in," she said hopefully.

The twins looked at each other. Saja nodded to Bruno. 'I'm going to explain to you, Bayley," he said. "She has an illness of the nerves, and this is not one of her good days. You must understand that she never feels safe. There are dark chapters in her life.

"In one prison camp under the Nazis, she watched her parents and her two sisters die. After the war was over, she and other survivors were trapped again, behind the Russians' barbed wire. She met my father in that camp in East Germany. They escaped together to Western territory.

"They were well treated, but it was still a camp, and they were kept there for seven years. We were born there. It was drab and hopeless—we don't remember very much, but we do remember the hopelessness.

"We were taken to England, and there we started to live, at last, like human beings. My father could forget the dark years because he was absorbed in his work, and Saja and I discovered what it was like to be happy. But our mother—she carried it all inside her, the pain and hunger and fear.

"When my father received the fine offer from this university, we hoped that putting an ocean between Mama and the past would help her. We think it will, eventually, but now it is too soon. That is why you must forgive when she seems rude."

"She doesn't seem rude at all!" Bayley exclaimed. "Can't you explain that I just came to be friendly? Oh dear, I wish my own mother was home. I wish I wasn't so clumsy and stupid!"

"She will come in," Bruno suddenly resolved. "Saja, I am going to bring her in."

Saja and Bayley waited. They heard a scuffling in the hall, a woman pleading. Bruno half-carried his mother in. Saja jumped up to pull out the chair across the table from Bayley, and Bruno kept his hand on his mother's arm, while his sister smoothed her hair, poured coffee and set a piece of cake before her. Saja pointed at Bayley, explaining, Bayley guessed, how a neighbor had come in friendship, and there was nothing to fear.

They heard the front door open, and Bruno said with relief, "It's Papa."

It seemed to Bayley that such a famous scientist ought to be about seven feet tall. She had caught glimpses of Dr. Sudak before, but now she had her first good look at him. He was rather short, rather insignificant in appearance. His thick glasses gave him the look of a stout brown owl.

He took in the situation at a glance. Saja said, "Papa, our friend came to call and brought a gift."

He went straight to his wife and kissed the top of her

untidy head. He cut a forkful of cake and put it to her lips as though she was a child. "Good," he said. "Jadwega, say 'good.' "

Mrs. Sudak said something that sounded like "goot," and her family beamed with pride. Then she took the fork and fed herself. She looked only at her plate, avoiding Bayley's glance.

A general conversation began, and Bayley, watching Mrs. Sudak without seeming to, noticed that her hand on the table, which had looked like a clenched claw, gradually loosened.

Bayley had wondered what she could ever find to say to a Nobel Prize winner. Now she discovered that she didn't have to make talk with the great Dr. Sudak. He was so interested in everything that he was an easy talker and listener.

He had observed the Hughes clan across the hedge. He had seen Chip and his pals tinkering in the yard. He was interested in Benjy's devotion to his car. He had become an admirer of Happy just from watching the Hughes dog. He inquired about Mr. Hughes, and Bayley explained that her father was the manager of an oil plant. This sounded pretty dull, but Dr. Sudak thought it a fascinating occupation.

Bayley found herself at ease and finally asked about the box of stones on the table. "That is my son's hobby," Dr. Sudak explained. "Bruno is a lover of rocks and minerals."

86

Bayley must have looked completely blank. How could anybody care about such homely rocks?

"I am considering majoring in geology," Bruno explained. "The area around Fenfield is extremely interesting from a geological point of view. Did you know that? Signs of the ice age are all around. I picked up these samples within a few miles of here."

Bayley took out one of the rocks. "What's this shiny stuff?"

"That's muscovite. What you probably call mica. A book in the college library describes local conditions, and tells of an abandoned mica mine. I located it and found some tourmaline crystals that are quite nicely faceted."

"That sounds like fun," Bayley said dubiously.

Bruno's face lit up as though she had cried, "Goodie! Lead me to it!"

"I'm going to try another locality in North Fenfield this Friday," he said. "I'd like it very much if you would come with me, Bayley."

This seemed like a pretty improbable kind of date, but it was the best offer Bayley had had in quite some time. A date to go rock hunting was better than sitting around biting her nails, she reflected, and politely accepted.

"I'd suggest you wear the dungarees you wear when you weed your mother's garden," he suggested. "We'll be scrambling down a cliff."

Bayley nodded and got up to go. She had an idea that formal calls were only supposed to last fifteen minutes, and she had stayed almost two hours. "Wait," Dr. Sudak said. "Before you go, Miss Bayley, I would like to try something. We'll keep talking, and will you move over to this side of the table and put your hand on my wife's shoulder? I think she is beginning to feel safe about you. This is the first time in years she has remained in the same room with a stranger. Gently now, my dear."

Bayley circled the table while the others carried on a conversation. Mrs. Sudak's eyes never left Bayley's face. When she stood in back of her, Bayley put her hand on her shoulder.

The sick woman trembled under her touch, and when she looked up Bayley gave her a warm smile. Slowly, Mrs. Sudak's hand crept out and covered Bayley's for a minute.

The doctor and his children went to the door to see Bayley off. "Thank you, my dear," he said. "Your visit has done us all a world of good."

"Can you be ready at one on Friday?" Bruno asked.

"Yes, but what do we use for a car?"

"We walk," Bruno said, then laughed. "Is that such a terrible idea? Don't Americans ever walk?"

Bayley bounced home on her toes, delighted with the success of her afternoon.

Now she had something concrete to report, when she wrote to her great-aunt that evening. "Dear Aunt Bayley," she began. "I took your advice and I am cultivating the family next door like mad. You were right, they are simply fascinating people.

88

"Tell Mother I baked them a cake and took it over, and it was good if I do say so as shouldn't!

"Jadwega Sudak, the mother, is ill. I mean, mentally ill, but she is quiet and timid. I intend to see her and be gentle with her, and find out if she will learn to trust me.

"Dr. Sudak is a real dear, simple and folksy. I thought he'd have his head in the clouds dreaming up all sorts of grim algebraic equations but he's not like that at all.

"I think Saja and I are going to be real friends, and tomorrow I'll ask her to go shopping with me. I have a good excuse as they don't have a cart like ours to carry packages in, so she can put her stuff in mine.

"Guess what? On Friday I have a date with Bruno. Doing what? Collecting rocks, that's what.

"So how'm I doin'? I'll report in full on this latest development when I write Mother on Sunday.

"Be a good girl, won't you, and do everything Mother and the doctor say? As one of your true admirers I look forward to seeing you out of that bed. Just think, you'll be just like a butterfly emerging from its chrysalis.

"How's that for a poetic simile? Ain't I gettin' learned? Your ever-lovin' namesake."

IX

"Sweetie, you'd like to take over the Sudaks lock, stock and barrel," Mr. Hughes warned Bayley. It was evening, and they were playing cribbage. He qualified the warning. "Your heart's in the right place, but you do rush into things. Think of friendship as a bird in a tree. It's a shy creature and has to be coaxed. You can't just shake the tree and expect it to drop in your lap."

"I know. I'm like a bulldozer," Bayley agreed.

Remembering her father's advice, she tried to avoid the bulldozer tactics the next time she saw Saja. They went to the store together, and it took them an hour to do their shopping because they had so much talking to do as they progressed along the aisles.

Bayley's impulse was to force the brightly packaged goods on her new friend, because the marvels of the supermarket were a revelation to Saja. "I've been here many times, but I didn't know what half of these things were," Saja confessed. She went on, "I wish I could make a good cake. The one you brought us was delicious. Papa and Bruno were so enthusiastic about it, they asked me to try to learn your secret."

"It's no secret," Bayley told her, leading the way to the ready-mix department. "These are all foolproof. You just add an egg and water, and presto! There you are." Maybe she sounded like a famous cake-maker from way back, but Bayley didn't feel it necessary to admit how recently she herself had learned how to bake.

On the way home, she mentioned, "I'd like to have you and your mother come for tea this afternoon."

Saja's intense young face had looked almost happy while they were exploring the store together, but now a shadow came over it. "That's kind of you, Bayley," she murmured, "but Mama doesn't go anywhere. I thought you understood that."

"But this isn't just anywhere," Bayley protested. "She seemed to like me. Remember how she let me hold her hand? I'd be quiet and easy with her, and I wouldn't let any of my brothers come roaring in to frighten her."

"Perhaps some time," Saja said. "She's not ready yet for such an adventure."

"Maybe you don't insist enough," Bayley said.

"Perhaps some day." Saja's tone cut off further argument.

"Will you come, then?"

"Yes."

"I'll have my friend Jean, too. She's anxious to meet you."

Saja made no answer.

"You've got to meet people," Bayley insisted. "You'll be starting school with us in September, and it will be ever so much easier if you know some of the kids. Jean won't bite. She's an awfully nice girl."

It turned out, though, that Jean was working that afternoon, taking care of a neighbor's children. It turned out, too, that it was just as well Saja didn't try to entice her mother to make the visit next door.

Saja came and was watching Bayley daintily arranging what Aunt Bayley would have called a "genteel collation." Bayley had baked brownies, having discovered a brownie mix on the magical shelf. Suddenly, Benjy and Chip and all Chip's motley crew materialized. They had noses like beagles for brownies. Saja looked absolutely terrified when the herd burst through the kitchen door. The only way Bayley could quiet them was by banging them over their heads with a rolled-up newspaper.

The younger boys concentrated on the food, but Benjy treated Saja with the respect he usually reserved for his elders. He didn't seem to realize she was his own age. Perhaps it was her dignity, and the grown-up way she wore her heavy braids, that put him off.

Bayley was dying to beg Saja to cut her hair, or fix it differently, before school started. But her new caution warned her to go slowly about giving such a personal suggestion.

The picture her father had evoked of the bird in the tree had made a real impression on Bayley. It seemed to her a workable attitude to adopt with other people in her life.

For instance, on the morning of her date with Bruno.

92

Jerry Flint unexpectedly appeared while she was hanging clothes. "Hi, Bay," he greeted her. "I came over to see if you'd play tennis."

This was the kind of invitation Bayley had been hoping for all summer. It hadn't been much fun, realizing all the swimming and tennis she was missing. The high-school crowd hung out at the Kampus Kitchen, but she hadn't yet been asked to join them. It wasn't that they disliked her, she knew. It was solely because she was new in the town, and they never gave her a thought.

Now Jerry was offering to open the door for her. He was a class officer, and if Bayley appeared at the school courts in his company, then automatically the crowd that hung out at the Kampus Kitchen would welcome her.

Once she would have blurted, "Oh gosh, Jerry, I can't, darn it. I have a date. But any afternoon next week I'd love to play." Now she said, "Oh, I'm so sorry, I have a date," and stopped.

He seemed taken aback. He said lamely, "I was supposed to play with Inky Bowman, but he folded up on me, and I thought of you."

Did he expect her to burst into paeans of gratitude because she was next on his list? Bayley guessed he did. She only remarked, laughing, "Every time you come, I seem to be wallowing in laundry, don't I?"

It was almost noon. When she went in, to fix soup and sandwiches for Chip, Jerry followed. She set three places and opened another can of soup.

Maybe she was wearing her worst beat-up dungarees

93

for the date with Bruno, but at least, Bayley reflected with satisfaction, she had really looked in the mirror when she combed her rusty thatch and made up her face. Jerry seemed to watch her with new interest as she capably moved around the kitchen.

Bayley had forgotten this was a day Benjy came home. She wasn't too happy to see him, for he disrupted a cozy little threesome. "Hurry up and eat," she ordered, planking the plate of sandwiches in front of him. "I've got a date."

"Where are you going?" Chip asked, his mouth full.

"I've told you, I'm going on a geological expedition with Bruno Sudak."

"What do you mean, a geological expedition?" Benjy demanded.

"I've told you a thousand times, we're going to gather samples," Bayley said with dignity.

"Samples of what?"

"Samples of rocks."

"Rocks?"

"Yes, rocks," she said, getting really annoyed now.

"Just plain old rocks?"

"There's nothing plain about a rock. What we're going for is to gather evidence of glacial periods. I don't suppose you know that this part of the country was once buried under ice." Bayley had learned by experience that a statement delivered in an authoritative voice could sometimes shut up her twin.

"I'd heard of it," Jerry put in, "but it happened before my time."

94

At that, Benjy reached over and gave Jerry a resounding bang on the back, to welcome him into the clan of Bayley-baiters.

"Yeah," Chip piped up, "old Bayley wouldn't know a glacier if it jumped out and bit her."

Bayley couldn't swing on Benjy because he would grab her arm and twist it until she yelled for help. However, there was no law that said she had to put up with sarcastic remarks from her smallest brother. She swung on Chip and her flat hand caught his ear. The result was a resounding slap, much harder than Bayley intended. Chip leaped up, full of fury. She had to apologize; she couldn't avoid it, because she had hit him much too hard.

The lunch ended in a shambles. Bayley stalked out, leaving the mess of dishes on the table, not even bothering to say good-bye to Jerry.

She was still fuming when she joined Bruno. He was carrying cloth sacks and a short-handled pick. They set off, and just the fact of walking soon burned away Bayley's anger. She had to step along smartly to match Bruno's long strides. They crossed the campus and reached the open country.

Bayley soon realized that Bruno was an easy kind of companion. She didn't have to give him a line, or act coy. He was properly solicitous and after a while inquired, "Would you like to stop and rest?"

"No," Bayley assured him, "I haven't quite lost the use of my legs yet. I suppose you think all the kids in this country are soft."

"I don't know many."

95

"I guess we are awfully dependent on cars, but there are a few of us who can get around under our own power. Maybe we're—we're—" Bayley frantically tried to think of the word.

"Anachronisms?"

"Yes, that's it."

They had reached the top of a hill, and Bruno stopped and shaded his eyes against the sun, looking back along the highway. Fenfield was hidden by trees, but they could make out the tall tower that housed the books of the university's library. Fields lay shimmering in the sun, and a red tractor pulling a hay baler made clanking noises that from a distance sounded oddly musical. "This is a beautiful land," Bruno murmured.

"I guess maybe it is." Bayley had never thought much about that.

Bruno was watching the baler toss neat squares of hay as it slowly circled the field. "If a farmer in my parents' country owned a machine like that, people would come many miles to marvel at it."

"What country do you mean?"

"Poland."

"I didn't know you'd ever been in Poland."

"My parents carry it with them wherever they go," Bruno said.

They went on. Bruno consulted a book he had borrowed from the library, which had maps showing how to find the mineral deposits in the locality. "North Fenfield pegmatite" was the one he was looking for. "If we both read it, we are less likely to miss the way," he suggested, passing the book to Bayley.

She read aloud, "Just beyond the railroad track on Route 37, take road bearing left and proceed up hill for 1.2 miles. Bear left at fork, cross small bridge. Entrance to mine on the right. Inquire at farmhouse for permission to visit."

"This is fun," Bayley said. "It's like following a map that leads to buried treasure. What are we going to find?"

"Mica and feldspar. If we're lucky we'll find garnet."

"Garnets!" Bayley exclaimed, walking faster.

"They won't be gem garnets," he cautioned. "There's another area described in the book where garnets in quantity have been gathered for commercial use. We'll go there another time, if you like. There's always a chance a good, clear stone will turn up."

"I think I've spent a wasted life!" Bayley exclaimed. "This is marvelous fun."

She was puffing, however, when they reached the top of the next hill. They were on a country road now, and under the trees the going was comfortable, but in the sun Bayley began to perspire. She pulled her shirt out and tied the tails around her waist to give her middle a little coolness. "We should have brought something to drink," she suggested.

"If we come to a clear-running brook, the water will be safe."

"We haven't anything to drink out of."

"We can drink from our hands," he said.

"Goodness, you certainly know a lot about nature."

Bruno bent a serious gaze on her. "That doesn't seem complicated," he said slowly. "Perhaps the feeling is stronger in me than in you, Bayley, that we all must learn the elemental things about how to survive."

"Why?" Bayley was startled by his seriousness.

"Because we never know at what moment our civilization will be swept away," was his unexpected answer.

The end of her own comfortable, slightly boring world seemed so remote to Bayley at that moment, she stared at him. "Oh, Bruno," she protested, "do you really believe that?"

He started to speak, then stopped. He looked at her as though she was no older than a child.

"That must be the farmhouse," Bayley said suddenly, glad to change the subject, "because here our road turns to the right. Let's ask."

They crossed a yard where squawking hens scattered at their approach, and knocked at the door. After a pause, it opened. A bent old man said through the crack, "What do you want?"

"May we have your permission to visit the mine, sir?" Bruno asked.

"Go ahead. You from the college?"

They nodded. Maybe they weren't exactly from the college, but in a couple of years they would be students there.

"Help yourselves. Be sure to put back the bars if you take 'em down, hear?"

They started along the path that led into the woods,

and soon reached the bars. A faded sign read, "Mine. Keep Out." Bayley promptly forgot she was a lady and got down on her stomach and slid under, although Bruno was preparing to help her over. A tumbledown shack attracted her, and she pushed aside tall weeds to look through the sagging door.

Bruno was turning rocks over on a rotting platform nearby. Bayley recollected that, although she had never encountered a snake, she would probably be scared out of her wits if she did, and hurried to join him.

They started up a sharp incline and then Bruno turned aside, drawn by a tumble of large boulders. Bayley watched him whacking away at them with his pick, but soon grew bored and wandered on, following a vague path upwards over rocks and moss. She was thinking: This nature stuff is all right; I like it.

The path stopped abruptly at the edge of a sharp drop. Bayley got down on her knees to peer over the edge of the sheer cliff. Fifty feet below, a tiny brook flowed into a green, scummy pool.

Bruno joined her and together they skirted the excavation until they found a place where they could clamber down. Recalling the possible presence of snakes, Bayley shrieked as they descended, hoping to scare them away.

The sun didn't penetrate to the bottom of the hole, but it was steamy and hot. Bruno looked about him with interest. He started explaining about things called gneiss and schist, spelling the words for Bayley's benefit.

Her mind began to wander. Finally she had to confess,

"I'm not taking any of it in, Bruno. I've got the kind of a mind that can't be stuffed too full. If I learn a new fact, then I have to forget something else to make room for it. Let's get on to the garnets. Where are they?"

Bruno pointed to a place on the rock face where a jagged angle of a different material cut across. "Maybe I'll find you some up there."

Bayley stumbled over loose stones to follow, but he warned, "Don't come any further." He climbed straight up and wrapped one arm around a pine tree which stuck out at an angle, its roots growing from what earth they found in a crack. Bayley watched him carefully tapping along the rock face. "I've found a few garnets, but they're not good ones," he called down. "There's fairly good tourmaline here."

Bayley was watching him worriedly, hoping he wasn't going to fall. Without thinking, she stepped back and suddenly she was tumbling. With a great crashing and yelling, she landed at the edge of the pool.

She pulled her feet out of the water and felt herself all over, to see what was broken. Her hand came away from her head with blood on it. She felt groggy, and her head hurt dully.

Bruno was at her side. "Stay where you are. Don't move," he ordered. He pushed away the scum to get clean water and wiped the dirt and blood from her forehead with his handkerchief. His face was white with anxiety. "It's only a surface cut, although I know it hurts badly," he said. He knelt beside her, absorbed in cleaning the wound, until the blood stopped running.

Bayley tried to laugh. "I'm all right. I don't mean to be such a baby. It was my own fault, not looking where I was going."

"Perhaps you'd better try to stand up." Bruno helped her to her feet. Bayley promptly sat down again, for the pain that shot through her ankle made her sick.

He removed her sneaker and felt the bones, then gently twisted the ankle. "I don't think anything is broken, but it's beginning to swell." His own hands were trembling. "I'm so terribly sorry that I've gotten us into this predicament."

"Well, the first thing to do is to get out of this hole," Bayley told him.

This time when she stood, Bruno held her firmly. She leaned against him for a moment, fighting the pain. With Bruno half-carrying her, they covered the distance to the cliff side.

"You'll never make the climb," Bruno said. "You'll have to wait here while I go for help."

"I will make it. I have to," Bayley told him, clenching her teeth. The prospect of being left alone in this steaming hole seemed much worse than tackling the cliff.

Somehow, with Bruno urging and supporting her, they climbed the rough incline, but they had to stop often to rest. They started down the path and the going became easier, for, with Bruno's arms around her, Bayley could hop on one leg. She kept her eyes closed as she fought down waves of nausea. At last, they reached the country road. Bruno seated her on the bank.

"I'll go and find a telephone," he said, starting away.

"I don't believe that old man has one. Look, Bruno, there aren't any telephone or power poles along this road."

"I'll get some water, anyway."

It was bliss just to rest on the soft grass. Bayley wished Bruno would never come back and she could lie there forever. But all too soon he returned, with water in a tin cup.

"You'll have to wait here. I'll go out to the main highway and find a telephone," he told her.

His narrow face was so full of concern that Bayley laughed weakly to reassure him. "This is awful," she croaked, "because you'll never take me again. My career as a geologist is over practically before it got started."

His face cleared and he said, "Do you mean you'll go with me again?"

"Of course I will. I can't let one sprained ankle cut short a promising career. Besides, I think the ankle feels better. If you'll help me, I'll make it to the main road with you."

They progressed in a hippity-hop manner and at last emerged on the busy highway. Bayley was contented to stay alone while Bruno ran a quarter-mile to the first house in view. He ran all the way back to tell her, "My father's on his way. He'll be here in a few minutes."

They waited in companionable silence. Bayley pulled grass and chewed the soft ends. A feeling was growing in her that she and Bruno Sudak were going to be real friends.

Dr. Sudak appeared and jumped out of his old black sedan. He knelt beside Bayley, and, while she was apologizing for all the trouble she was causing, he studied her ankle, gently feeling it. "There's nothing broken. I hope it's just a bad sprain."

"My father is a medical doctor, too," Bruno explained.

"We won't take any chances, however," Dr. Sudak said. "We'll have it X-rayed before we take you home."

They helped Bayley to the car, and Dr. Sudak drove to the college infirmary. Dr. Driscoll, the college physician, X-rayed the ankle, and when the picture was developed he assured Bayley that no bones were broken or misplaced, and that she would be all right at home. He taped the ankle, and, when Bayley put her weight on it, she discovered that the pain was much easier.

When they drove up in front of the Hughes house, the whole family poured out to meet them. It wasn't until then that Bayley realized that the shadows had lengthened and the day was almost gone.

Now she had six men to assist her into the house. Benjy remarked cheerfully, "She did it on purpose to get out of cooking dinner."

Tom picked her up and carried her to her own room. She could hear her father and Dr. Sudak talking in the living room below. Then, as the Sudaks were leaving, she heard Bruno say, "May I call on your daughter tomorrow, sir, to find out how she is?"

Mr. Hughes said heartily, "Don't stand on ceremony, son. Come over any time. Thanks for taking such good care of my girl."

Bayley managed to undress. At last, she reached the sanctuary of her own bed, and it felt like heaven. Chip came pounding up the stairs to shout, "Who's going to cook our dinner?"

Benjy caught up with him and hauled him away. "Lay off it," he ordered. "Give her a break."

Mr. Hughes took charge then and fed the boys and heated soup and made toast and brought a tray to Bayley.

They let her feel like a pale, interesting heroine. They waited on her all evening, so thoughtfully and solicitously that Bayley realized they could be pretty darned nice when they tried.

X

As LUCK WOULD HAVE IT, that very evening Mrs. Hughes called. Chip, who reached the telephone first, blurted, "Bayley broke her ankle."

Mr. Hughes said quickly, "Bayley sprained her ankle, Elizabeth, but she's all right. We're getting along fine, and there's nothing to worry about."

"My poor baby," Mrs. Hughes, must have said, for Bayley heard Chip's retort, "Poor baby nothing! She's sitting up in bed acting like Mrs. Astor's pet horse."

"Shut up, twerp." Tom yanked the phone away from him.

As a result of that conversation, the next day a taxi stopped in front of the house, and Mrs. Hughes came in quietly. She was halfway up the stairs when Bayley, hopping along the hall to the bathroom, saw her. It was such a wonderful shock that Bayley almost fell down the stairs to meet her.

She helped Bayley back to bed and looked at the ankle, which was turning nicely black and blue above and below the strapping. She tidied the room, and then the two had a good talk.

"How long can you stay?" Bayley wanted to know.

"Just until tomorrow. Aunt Bayley's friend Emma moved into the apartment to take my place. She has to go to work on Monday, so I'll have to be back Sunday night. It's a tiny visit, but Aunt Bayley insisted that I come home."

Bayley had fast hold of her mother's hand. "Then I wish you'd stay in this very spot all the time."

"I'll stay in this very spot until Dad and the boys come," her mother assured her.

Bayley dreaded having her see the house. She was trying to recall how it had looked yesterday morning, before she set off with Bruno. The laundry basket, she remembered now, was overflowing. She hadn't even started the Friday cleaning, thinking, What difference does it make? I can clean all weekend. And the kitchen must be a shambles. She hadn't been near it since she walked out, leaving Chip to cope with yesterday's lunch dishes.

She confessed, "Mother, I'm ready to die thinking what a mess you'll find. You've got to take my word for it—usually the house looks better."

"Of course I believe you, dear," her mother answered placidly.

Chip arrived home first and hearing two women's voices, came to investigate. "Oh boy, Ma, am I glad you're home!"

He seized her in a bear hug until she protested, "You'll crack my ribs, Chip!"

Bayley was seeing her mother with new eyes. Didn't she seem thinner, paler? A pang shot through Bayley as

106

she realized: Mother's pretty darned precious, and we take her for granted.

Chip plainly showed his pleasure as his mother drew him to her. "You're not too big to do a little smooching with your mother," she said, hugging her youngest.

To cover his pleased embarrassment, Chip said gruffly, "Old Bayley went and broke her ankle just to get out of doing the work."

Bayley was in no mood to resent anything, but gave Chip the glowering look he expected. "I don't believe old Bayley sprained her ankle on purpose," Mrs. Hughes said. "But now I've got to go down and case the joint. Chip, come with me. You'll probably have to go to the store."

Bayley heard them below stairs, her mother's cheerful tones accompanying Chip's happy chatter. She heard the vacuum cleaner's whine, yet it was her mother who came upstairs. "Don't tell me he's helping you clean!" Bayley said. "He'd run for his life if I suggested such a thing."

"I learned long ago that, no matter how old a man is, you have to use what Benjy calls 'the old oil' on him," her mother answered. "Vinegar's just no use on anything that wears pants."

The doorbell rang, and Mrs. Hughes called down to Chip to answer it, but by now he was burning papers in the back yard, so she went down. Bayley heard, "Excuse me. I am Bruno Sudak."

"Oh yes!" Mrs. Hughes exclaimed, "you're Bayley's friend. I'm her mother. Come in."

"I came to inquire how she is and to bring her the

107

garnets we found. I'm so sorry, Mrs. Hughes. It was my fault she was hurt."

Bayley, listening, felt warm happiness floood through her. Sometimes the family kidded Mrs. Hughes about the way she used her charm to make life pleasant for everybody, but Bayley appreciated it now, hearing her using it on Bruno. "I know that just isn't so," Mrs. Hughes said. "I think you and your father must have handled Bayley's little accident splendidly. In fact, it's our great good luck that your father is a doctor. We haven't lived in town long enough to find a family doctor yet. Wouldn't you like to go up and give Bayley the garnets?"

Bruno was apparently nonplused by this informality. "Do you think I ought to?"

"I certainly do," Mrs. Hughes assured him, and called, "Bayley, there's a visitor on his way. Second door on your left, Bruno."

His face was crimson with embarrassment when he appeared, and Bayley laughed. "Come in, I won't bite. Haven't you ever called on a lady in her boudoir before?"

"I brought the garnets." He laid in Bayley's hand some small objects which looked like pebbles and yet had an unmistakable dark red tinge.

"They're nice! Was that what you were digging out of the rock when I fell?"

"Yes. I told you we probably wouldn't find gem stones, but these are real garnet. If your parents will allow you to go with me again, we'll try the other place I told you of. We might find clearer, larger stones."

"Of course, they'll let me, just as soon as I can stand on this stupid ankle. And don't you try to take the blame for that, Bruno. It was entirely my own fault. I stepped back without looking."

He seemed uneasy, ready to run. Bayley kept the conversation loud and matter-of-fact, until it was time for him to go.

Her father came in as Bruno was leaving, and soon Tom and Benjy arrived, and Bayley felt left out of the hullabaloo downstairs. Then the whole tribe trooped up to do their visiting with their mother around Bayley's bed, where she could enjoy it, too.

Chip repeated his remark about old Bayley breaking her ankle on purpose, but Benjy promptly smothered him in a pillow. Bayley lay back and watched their faces. Her father's shone with happiness, and he couldn't keep his eyes off her mother. Bayley realized he'd never stopped missing her for a minute.

Presently Mrs. Hughes remarked, "Bayley has some interesting garnets to show for her adventure."

Bayley took the precious pebbles out of her pajama pocket. She saw with satisfaction how impressed the men were when she learnedly spoke about strata in rocks and facets in stones. "How did you pick up all that jazz?" Benjy demanded, startled that she knew so much.

Now that their mother was home, everything went well. The next day, Bayley spoke about that to her father. She had hopped downstairs to be with people. Her bedroom seemed lonely. "How come everything runs so much

109

better and the boys are so much nicer?" she asked her father, who was contentedly doing odd carpentry chores for her mother.

"The whole house sings," he mused.

"Yes, that's it."

Late in the afternoon, however, Mrs. Hughes prepared to go back to Brentford. Nobody tried to argue her out of going. "You seen your duty and you're doing it," Tom said slangily.

She helped Bayley upstairs and tucked her into a freshly made bed. She had saved a few minutes for a private little talk. "Just a short argy-bargy," she warned, settling down in the chintz-covered chair, a bit of last-minute darning in her hands.

Bayley put the same question to her. "Dad says that when you're home, Mom, the whole house sings. How come? Honestly, I try to do my best, but sometimes the place looks like a magpie's nest."

"I know that often you children think that Mama's poems are really square," her mother answered, "but as usual I have a little one to suit the occasion. Would you like to hear it?"

"I guess so," Bayley said doubtfully.

Her mother laughed, and went on:

" 'Order is a lovely thing.
On disarray it lays its wing,
Teaching simplicity to sing.
It has a meek and lowly grace,

Quiet as a nun's face.
Lo—I will have thee in this place!'

"Maybe most people have forgotten that poem of Anna Hempstead Branch's," Mrs. Hughes finished, "but you'd find it useful. Would you like me to write it out for you?"

"Yes, and I'll learn it, and maybe it might do some good. Mother—"

"Yes, dear?"

"I've been thinking about something."

"Yes, dear."

"Well, I've been wondering why I'm so skinny. I mean, I'm so flat. You're so nice and bosomy, but look at me. What have I got? The other girls are developing, but I'm not. Oh, I suppose it's silly, but I look in the mirror and jeepers, what do I see? A great big nothing."

"I don't believe there's anything wrong with your health, and maybe any minute you'll start to sprout," her mother said comfortingly. "But if it worries you we'll make an appointment with the doctor, the next time I come home."

Now that she had foisted this problem off on her mother, Bayley felt better immediately. "When will you be home for good?"

"In a few weeks. Aunt Bayley's due to 'emerge from her chrysalis,' as you elegantly put it, in a few days. She'll walk around in the apartment. Then I'll stay until she gets back her strength, so she can take care of herself. She has such an iron will, that may not take long."

"Mother—"

"What, Bayley? I really have to go."

Bayley blurted, "Mother, what do people do about being lonely?"

Her mother didn't brush that off. The obvious answer was "Nonsense! What have you got to be lonely about?" Instead, she said gently, "Does that bother you very often, Bayley?"

"No, not often," Bayley said honestly, "and the boys and Dad are pretty darn marvelous. It's just once in a while."

"I'll tell you what I do. I just get busy with the first thing that comes to hand, and soon I lose myself in that, and the feeling goes away."

Mr. Hughes was calling from the front hall.

"Now I've got to go," Bayley's mother said, folding the darned socks. "Write and tell me what else is on your mind, darling." She stooped for a quick kiss and was gone.

XI

Tom had a date with his Beth. The other boys and Mr. Hughes had takenMrs. Hughes to the station. The house, usually alive with noises large and small, was very quiet. Bayley lay in her comfortable bed, listening to the silence. Happy wandered upstairs, looking for some cheerful society, and flopped onto the rug, sighed, and slept.

The men came home, paid brief calls to see that Bayley had everything she needed, and straggled off to their rooms.

She caught her father's hand to hold onto him. "Dad, I'll flip if I have to stay here much longer. Won't you talk to that Dr. Driscoll at the infirmary, to find out if I can get up and do things?"

"I'll call him in the morning before I go to work," Mr. Hughes promised. "I want to tell him how much we appreciate his taking care of you. He did it as a favor to Dr. Sudak, but we still owe him a 'thank you.' Go to sleep now, Punkin."

But sleep would not come. For the first time in her life, Bayley had a real bout of insomnia. She had nothing very

113

serious or important on her mind. All was well in her world, wasn't it? Yet she couldn't drop off to sleep.

Maybe being lonely once in a while is a part of growing up, she thought. It didn't seem a very good part. She tried counting sheep and then tried counting her blessings: good parents, a comfortable home, a mess of brothers who weren't so terribly awful, friends, health. She told herself sharply: Don't you feel sorry for yourself; you've got no excuse.

Finally she turned on the light and tried to read *Rocks and Minerals,* the book Bruno had loaned her. Benjy, looking at it, had renamed it "How to Tell Your Friends from the Rocks." It wasn't exactly a fascinating book, but it did its job and lulled her to sleep.

Her father came in the next morning to tell her, "I talked with Dr. Driscoll, and he said you could get up and do what you want to within reason, but to rest frequently during the day. He asked about your head. Does that feel all right?"

"Oh, sure."

"You can putter around, then, but take it easy." He kissed her absently, his mind on the day's work awaiting him at his office.

She hobbled downstairs. Chip was making some clumsy attempts to clear up the kitchen. He was so gratified when she took his place at the sink he made no objection to any of the chores she assigned him such as emptying the garbage and burning the papers.

Bayley took frequent rests and realized that the pain was almost gone, that her ankle ached dully only when she stood too long. She limped around the rooms seeing them with new eyes, observing all the little things her mother had done to set the house straight. Mother is house-proud, she thought, and that's not a bad thing to be. Maybe, if I get the hang of it better, I'll begin to be house-proud, too.

Benjy was due to come home for lunch, and Bayley decided to surprise him. She consulted her faithful cookbook and beat up a batch of waffles.

He, too, seemed delighted to find his sister busy and waiting for him, instead of suffering and lolling in her bed. "This is a bit of all right," he said, tucking into the feast. "Ye gods, it was a pain in the neck having you laid up."

" 'Ye gods' is right," she agreed.

When a few days had passed, her ankle was as good as new, except for the bruise, which lingered colorfully. Bruno went geologizing alone, but he assured her he was saving the sand bank where the garnets were for their next trip.

Saja came one afternoon at Bayley's invitation; Bayley was beginning to despair that either Sudak would catch on to the idea of dropping in casually. Saja was dressed in a way that would have suited her mother, at least as far as age went. Where would anybody get an outfit like that? Bayley wondered. The dress was dark-blue silk, with a round neck embroidered with beads, and it hung ungracefully on Saja's thin figure. Her lips were without lipstick.

Not long ago—at the beginning of this summer, in fact —Bayley might have blurted out what she thought: "Saja, we've got to do something about your hair. It makes you look about a hundred and ten years old. Saja, how about us going shopping together? You'd look marvelous in toreador pants." Now Bayley held her tongue.

She was wary, afraid of frightening off this shy bird or, rather, this shy deer. Saja made her think of the does at the animal farm she had visited with her father, not the bold ones who had put their slim feet on her shoulders demanding a treat, but the timid ones who had stayed in the background.

Talking with Saja, Bayley glimpsed the depth and richness of the other girl's background, and realized there were dark places there, also. But when, in the long silences that occurred in their conversation, she saw the wistful look in Saja's dark eyes, Bayley longed to find the right words that would let the girl relax and accept friendship. She needs to let her hair down in more ways than one, Bayley guessed.

This problem came up again on a day when Bayley went shopping with Jean. Jean was going to the shore for a week and needed a couple of new dresses. They found summer sales, and Bayley could afford to be a spendthrift, because she had saved fifteen dollars out of her allotment without skimping on her family's food.

They took a long time poking around Fenfield's stores and were walking along Main Street, trying to decide which dresses to buy of those they had tried on, when Bayley saw Saja ahead, approaching them.

She took Jean's arm. "There's Saja Sudak now. You two have never met. Come on!"

Saja looked up, saw Bayley and Jean hurrying toward her, and darted into a doorway.

Bayley stopped short. "Why did she do that? I'm positive she saw us. Why should she be mad at me? Come on, let's go in that store and find her."

Jean hung back. "No," she said. "If she doesn't want to talk to us, that's her business, and you ought not to force her."

Astonished, Bayley demanded, "Aren't you mad because she doesn't want to meet you? She'd have stopped if I'd been alone; I'm pretty sure of that."

"You don't understand much about shy people," Jean said. "I had a dose of it once, and I know. Maybe you won't believe it, but I was so scared of people I'd cross the street rather than meet them and have to say 'Hello.' "

"I don't believe it," Bayley said flatly. "You're the least timid person I know."

"I got over it," Jean told her. "I knew I had to, so I did. It was just a temporary thing. I guess it started because I had such an awful time for a while with my complexion. My face was a mess, all broken out."

They walked on, turned into the big department store, and bought the dresses a patient clerk had put away for them earlier. Bayley was still musing over this new insight she had been given into Jean's nature. People are the most surprising things in the world, she concluded.

Bayley was still brooding over the strangeness of human nature, as she and Jean ate hot fudge sundaes, when Jean brought up the subject again. "Try once more to get the three of us together," she suggested. "We've got to do something about Saja's clothes before school starts, that's for sure. If she looks like that all the time, she'll be set down for a freak."

Bayley did try again, and succeeded one day when she was waiting for Jean to drop in. The afternoon was so hot that the streets shimmered, the house baked, and even under the tree in the back yard no breeze stirred the heavy air. Happy had dug himself a cool hole under the hydrangeas, and Bayley didn't have the heart to drag him out and fill up the hole.

Saja emerged from her back door. Bayley wore short shorts and a Basque shirt. Saja was again wearing what must have been one of her mother's cotton print dresses, stockings, of all things, and sensible shoes. Bayley called, "Come on over!"

Saja's face lit up, but she said doubtfully, "I don't think I should."

"Oh, come on!"

"Just for a minute, then. I'll make sure Mother is all right."

They had settled in lawn chairs when they heard someone walking through the house calling, "Hello, hello!"

Saja started up. Bayley caught her arm. "Don't run away. It's only my girl friend." She was holding Saja by force when Jean came across the grass to join them.

Jean paid no attention to Saja beyond a polite "Hello, how are you?" in response to Bayley's introduction. She talked about the weather, about Happy, about a book she had been reading, about anything under the sun which was impersonal. Saja gradually relaxed and leaned back in the wicker chair. She still had a wary look, but she wasn't trying to run away.

Bayley noticed that, as always, Mrs. Sudak was hovering at her kitchen window, watching the girls in the next yard.

"Bay, you said once you wanted to know how to make Italian spaghetti," Jean mentioned. "Did you get the stuff I told you to buy? We could make it now if you want to have it for dinner tonight."

Bayley started to argue, "It's too hot."

Jean ignored that. "Come on in the kitchen."

She set Bayley to chopping onions, while she fried a piece of garlic in olive oil and started tomato sauce bubbling on the stove. "Bayley's one of our high-school egg-heads," she explained to Saja," with no time to take a sensible course like home ec. The poor guy she marries will probably be regaled with the latest news about modern poetry while she heats up canned beans for him. Benjy says you're doing better, though, Bay."

119

"I think Bayley is an excellent cook," Saja said earnestly. She didn't yet understand about kidding; she took everything that was said literally.

"I'll bet you could give us some good recipes," Jean suggested. "Have you learned Polish cooking from your mother?"

"Yes, but we are learning the foods of your country."

"You ought to show us how to make some things that are purely Polish," Jean said positively. Or rather, show me. Your lessons would be wasted on Bayley."

"I will if you wish," Saja agreed doubtfully.

Jean went right on, "What's the point of living in a melting pot like the good old U.S.A. if we don't learn new things? Now, maybe there are some things you'd like to know before you start school. Oh, we have a lot of quaint customs you might not catch on to right away."

Was it a look of hope Bayley glimpsed in Saja's dark eyes? However, Saja said only, "That is true."

"You've got a marvelous lot of hair," Jean said. "It's beautiful. How long is it? I bet it's long enough to sit on."

"Yes, it is."

"Well, show us."

"I couldn't do that!" Saja protested.

"Why not? We're just three girls together. It's a good chance for all of us to let down our hair."

Saja looked blank, and Jean laughed. "That's an American expression. It means relax, take it easy, say what's on our minds."

Saja reluctantly began taking out the big pins that held her braids in a coronet, and a cascade of rippling dark hair covered her shoulders and fell below her waist. She tossed it back from her face. "I don't know what to do with it," she confessed. "I have studied on the street the way girls arrange their hair, but this is the way my mother taught me. And my father takes pride in it."

"Would he have a fit if you cut it?" Bayley asked.

"No. Papa says we may do what we wish to Americanize ourselves. No, he would not be angry."

"Would you like to cut it?"

"I would dearly love to."

"Let's!" Bayley exclaimed.

"Now?" Saja looked panicky.

"Yes, now."

Jean vetoed that. "Use your head, Bayley," she said. "If we took the scissors to it, we'd send Saja home looking like a freak. We'll make an appointment with a good hairdresser, Saja. He'll invent a hairdo for you that will suit your face. And I daresay he'll sell your hair for you, if you don't want to keep it. I know a woman who got fifty dollars for hair that was no longer or finer than yours."

All this time, Jean had proceeded with her cooking, making meatballs and boiling spaghetti. Her remarks to Saja were made in an offhand way, as though she wasn't too vitally interested. Bayley, who had been considerably taken aback by how much she was accomplishing, suddenly perceived the skill of Jean's method. How does she know so much about handling people? Bayley wondered. How could I have thought Jean was just a lightweight? I pigeonholed her without really knowing her at all.

Jean said briskly, "Is there any other way we can help you, Saja, about getting ready for school? I know if I was in your shoes, I'd be simply petrified, facing a new school, in a new town, in a new country."

"Saja went to school in England," Bayley pointed out, "and that can't have been too different."

"But it was!" Saja exclaimed. "It's like night and day, it's so different, the way you talk, the way you comport yourselves—I mean, the way you act—the way you dress."

"You'll get used to the way we talk and act," Jean said, "although I can't imagine why anybody would want to copy us. I've always heard that Americans use the worst slang and have the worst manners in the world—"

"No, no, no!" Saja interrupted vehemently. "Your manners are beautiful, so friendly and warm."

Jean went on, "As for the way we dress, well, I do think we dress sensibly, and that would be the easiest thing in the world to teach you. Good heavens, that's just a matter of buying a few clothes. Then you'd look just like us, if that's what you want."

Bayley caught her breath. She had been longing to take Saja in hand, to march her to a store and buy her skirts and blouses and Bermudas, and sandals for Saja's poor feet, which were always encased in heavy shoes. Jean had crashed that barrier.

How was Saja going to take this, though? Jean had

gone too far. She had entirely disregarded the pride of this intelligent, serious girl.

Saja murmured, "Papa has tried to make me buy new clothes, but I didn't know what I needed. I didn't even know what to ask for. And I couldn't wear what you do!" she burst out. "My legs—"

"What's the matter with them?" Jean demanded. "You've got lovely legs."

"But they are too long!"

"No, they're not. You'll look stunning in shorts, with a blouse or a shirt that fits you."

"But I'm too thin, too flat."

Bayley exclaimed, "You're worried about being flat? Look at me!"

Jean jumped in to turn Bayley's remark to her advantage. "Yes," she said. "I'm not insulting you, Bay, but Saja has a lot better figure. Of course, it's just too bad neither of you is as well endowed as I am. But that's just the breaks, kid," she finished, giving Bayley a friendly push to show she meant no offense.

"Skip it," Bayley said, getting into the spirit of the occasion. "I've got to get some things for school, too, and I'll tap my old man—what I mean is, Saja, I'll ask my father—for some dough. I mean, money. How about tomorrow?"

They made a date to spend the next afternoon shopping. Saja, looking anxious and hopeful at the same time, excused herself and went home.

By mutual consent, Bayley and Jean refrained from

talking about her after she had gone. Jean only said, as she was leaving, "I like her."

"You did a simply terrific job, leading her around, bringing her out," Bayley said appreciatively. "I still can't figure out how you did it, though."

"Maybe it was easier because I was the outsider," Jean said. "You know, bull in the china shop and all that. I'll see you tomorrow."

XII

IT WAS FUNNY how one thing led to another. It was really pretty interesting how things worked out.

For instance, that very evening, when Mr. Hughes was trimming his wife's rose border and clipping off the dead blossoms, Dr. Sudak made a point of crossing the yard to speak to him. Bayley saw them out there puffing on their pipes and talking. When her father came in, she asked what they had talked about for so long.

"He's grateful for what you're doing for his daughter," Mr. Hughes told her. "He said he'd hoped that his girl would be accepted as one of the crowd, and that he could see the start of that. He gives you all the credit. He admires you tremendously, Punkin."

"What else did you talk about?"

"Oh, about business."

"Does he know anything about business?"

"He's interested in the chemistry end of the petroleum industry."

"Did you ask him what he got the Nobel Prize for?"

"Good grief, no! What if I had and he'd told me? I

would really have exposed my ignorance. As it was, a lot of the things he said went way over my head.

"I got the impression that all of them, he and his children, have a real passion for learning for its own sake. That's quite different from the attitude of a lot of people, that education is only a means to an end, a way to make money, to get somewhere."

"You liked him?"

"I certainly did, and your mother will, too. It seems that he's done some work on a new formula for plant growth, and he wants to try it out on her roses. He's going to bring some over, and we'll see how it works."

The next afternoon Bayley and Saja met Jean at Thompson's Department Store. Saja's eyes were bigger than ever in her thin face; she was wearing what Bayley thought of as her "frightened fawn" look. Walking downtown, she had confided how pleased Dr. Sudak was that the girls were going to turn her into a typical high-school student.

"No," Bayley protested, "we don't want you to look like us. That would be awful! We just want you to be comfortable."

"He understands that." Saja's chuckle was throaty and musical.

"My father's pretty keen about your father," Bayley said. "He's hoping we can surprise my mother with roses as big as saucers, when she comes home."

"Botany was my mother's field," Saja mentioned.

"It was?" This really stopped Bayley short. Who would

ever think of unkempt, hysterical Jadwega Sudak as a
student? Saja must mean that her mother had studied
before the war, before the tragedy began, Bayley assumed.
She realized that she must try sometime to lead Saja into
talking about her mother. This was another interesting
piece of the Sudak puzzle.

Saja almost lost her nerve when the girls marched her
into the beauty parlor on the mezzanine at Thompson's.
They handed her over to Philip, who usually cut their
hair. They insisted on going into the booth, for each had
her own idea of how Saja ought to look.

Philip admiringly combed out the dark, lustrous hair,
letting it fall through his clever fingers. "You're absolutely sure you want to have it cut, Miss?"

Saja gripped the arms of the chair. "Yes, please go
ahead."

"I think it should be real short with some curls on top,"
Jean said positively.

"No," Bayley contradicted, "brush it back and curl
the ends so it hangs down. Saja's too tall for a lot of hair
on top."

"You're both leaving," Philip announced.

"What are you going to do to her?"

"That is purely my concern and Miss Sudak's. Out,
out!" he cried, waving the scissors at them.

They wandered around town looking in windows until two hours had passed, then returned to the beauty
salon. Philip was removing the big apron which swathed

Saja, and one of the other operators was carefully wrapping the cut tresses in tissue paper. Saja was staring at herself in the mirror, touching her hair wonderingly.

"I lost my courage," Philip confessed. "Perhaps your friend is not in the height of fashion, but this becomes her."

He had shaped Saja's hair in a long, loosely waved page-boy cut, falling to her shoulders. The top was smooth and shining, shaping her face like a frame.

Saja's eyes were happy as they met Bayley's. "You look ten years younger!" Bayley exclaimed. She wanted to add, "And you look absolutely beautiful."

Because Saja did. She seemed their own age, and yet she seemed different. She had a distinguished air.

Philip had left them alone. "Do I tip him?" Saja asked.

"Yes, give him a dollar. He did a marvelous job," Jean told her.

Bayley noticed that Saja walked taller, with new confidence, as they progressed through the store. Her shyness came back while they were shopping, for the clerks intimidated her. Jean and Bayley stuck like burrs, making sure the dresses, blouses, and sandals she bought were really what she wanted.

One shirtwaist dress of cornflower blue was so becoming that Bayley suggested, "Don't take it off. Wear it today." She bought a choker of inexpensive white beads and put it around Saja's neck. Saja protested, and Bayley said, "It's nothing, just a tiny present from me to you."

She and Jean were so proud of their handiwork, they

loaded up with boxes and carried everything home. Bayley was longing to see what would happen when Saja's family first glimpsed the transformation. She would have loved to insist that she and Jean go in, too, but a new sensitivity stopped her. They piled the boxes in Saja's arms, while she poured out her gratitude.

When Dr. Sudak came down the walk to help with the packages, Saja said meekly, "Do you like me, Papa?"

He kissed her cheek. "I think I have a new daughter. I like her very much."

Bayley and Jean walked on. "They can't ask us in on account of the mother," Bayley explained. The girls parted with the warm feeling that they had done a good day's work.

That evening, Tom utterly confounded Bayley by announcing, "Sis, I'd like to ask Beth here for supper Saturday night, if that's okay with you."

She was so startled she stammered, "Why sure, ask her if you want to. But once before when I suggested it, you turned a livid green at the thought of Beth eating my cooking."

"You've improved since then. As a matter of fact, that spaghetti you made yesterday was as good as any I've ever eaten. How about making that?"

"Okay." Bayley didn't think it necessary to destroy Tom's impression that she had blossomed into a culinary genius by telling him it was Jean who had made the spaghetti. She had watched carefully; Jean had shown her each step of the process; and by now she had learned enough to cook up a fair imitation. In any case, she could telephone Jean for help if she got stuck. "What else do you want me to make?" she asked.

"How about a nice tossed salad? But don't fix any dessert. I'll get some spumoni at the Italian place downtown."

Bayley couldn't help but be flattered. The fact that Tom would let his beloved risk her health by eating his sister's cooking showed remarkable new confidence. Bayley proceeded to give the house a better cleaning than its usual weekly lick and a promise. She was planning to arrange lots of flowers and do everything she could to make Tom's home seem a nice one.

On Friday, however, a letter came that made Tom's party lose some of its importance. "Bayley, would you like a change of scene?" her mother wrote. "Your aunt is doing so well she can spare me for a bit, so how about our changing jobs? Dad could drive you over and take me home for a week, and the following Sunday we'd change back again. After that I'll stay here only two weeks, or three at most, and then I'll come home to stay."

It wasn't too flattering, the way the men's faces lit up when they learned their women were swapping jobs. Benjy made a crack about Aunt Bayley suffering a relapse under his sister's care. Tom asked, "How about tomorrow night? Is it still all right for Beth to come?"

"Of course," Bayley told him.

The boys helped her set their mother's flower border to

rights, and cut the grass and trimmed the hedge and filled up all the holes Happy had dug. He had done extensive excavating during the summer months. Bayley put in a busy Saturday, accomplishing an enormous number of tasks and at the same time hovering over the spaghetti sauce bubbling on the stove.

The dinner party was a resounding success. The house looked serene and attractive and the dinner was delicious, if Bayley "said so herself as shouldn't." Beth turned out to be an easy guest, who entered into the spirit of the house. She smiled at the way the boys kidded their sister, and at the same time came out resoundingly on Bayley's side. Happy made quite a fool of himself over her, and that, of course, endeared her to the Hughes tribe.

Beth helped Bayley until the last dish was washed and the last pot put away, while Tom leaned in the door, practically drooling, plainly showing his pride in his sister and his appreciation of the domestic side of his girl.

On Sunday, Mr. Hughes and Chip drove Bayley to Brentford. Aunt Bayley was waiting for him in her chair by the window, where she had been watching the street for the first sight of their car. Now she was able to get around with the aid of a cane.

"Your job is to sit on her," Mrs. Hughes instructed Bayley. "She feels so good and she's so full of pep she'll try to put things over on you, such as setting out on ten-mile hikes. I hope you didn't come for a rest, child. It's all anyone can do to keep up with your aunt."

While Aunt Bayley talked to Chip, Mr. Hughes led his wife out to the kitchenette. "Is she really as chipper as she looks and acts?"

"She really is," Mrs. Hughes said. "The therapist from the hospital has been coming twice a week to give her exercise. Isn't it wonderful? In the old days she would have been kept in a cast for months, and it would have taken more weary months to get her on her feet. The way they put a pin in a fractured hip today is a magical sort of a business."

Then Mrs. Hughes drew Bayley to her. "Dear, my real reason for asking you to come was because your friendship means so much to her. I think her accident made her begin to question her own immortality for the first time. Before that, I believe your great-aunt actually planned on living forever! Her accident scared her, and the people she loves seem doubly precious to her now. You seem to be very high on her list of favorite people."

This confidence of her mother's gave Bayley a warm glow around her heart, as she stood in the window waving good-bye to her family.

As soon as they were gone, Aunt Bayley energetically jerked her chair around to face the room. "What do you want to do?" Bayley asked, smiling down at her.

"I want to make hay," her aunt said. "Your ma has kept me down long enough. Let's have a party."

"What kind of a party?"

"Let's have a cocktail party. We'll ask all the girls in and make whoopee."

The thought of Aunt Bayley's schoolteacher friends congregating over cocktails and making whoopee strained Bayley's imagination. "Aunt Bayley, you never drank a cocktail in your life. You don't even know what a cocktail is."

Her aunt sighed. "I can see you're going to be just as stuffy as my last nurse. Get out the cribbage board. I'll see if your pa's taught you anything about the game. Not that he knows anything about it. If I couldn't beat the pants off Ben Hughes, I'd be ashamed of myself."

They spent the evening over the cribbage board, and Bayley discovered that her father had been a careless teacher indeed. No matter how good her cards were, Aunt Bayley's pegs moved up and down the board with lightning rapidity. "You're making up new rules as you go along!" Bayley accused.

"Nonsense. The rules are as ancient as the law of the Medes and Persians. My father was the champion cribbage player of this town, if not of this state, and he taught me when I was no bigger 'n a tadpole."

"Aunt Bayley, I know you cheat," her niece said in despair at the end of the evening, as she totted up the score.

"Did you catch me at it?"

"No."

"Well, then!" her aunt crowed. "Now help me to bed."

"Did you cheat?"

"That's for me to know and you to find out."

Bayley soon learned that her housekeeping duties were

133

light. Aunt Bayley and the doctor saw eye to eye on the matter of her keeping active. She insisted on taking a hand with the household chores, propping herself at the sink to wipe the few dishes as Bayley washed.

Bayley discovered, however, that her social duties were something else again. The telephone rang all day long. A steady stream of callers came, and the small, sunny apartment was filled with chatter, while Bayley made innumerable pots of strong tea.

One day, Aunt Bayley had a suspiciously bright gleam in her eye, and finally she let the cat out of the bag. "We're having a real party tonight."

"Who says so? Aunt Bay, I'm not a good enough cook to entertain your friends."

"It's all arranged. It's a catered party. What do you think of that?"

"Now wait a minute! Slow down."

"You'll see," her aunt promised. "You know my most intimate friend, Georgianna Morgan? Of course you do. You struggled through Latin with her last year, before you moved to Fenfield, didn't you? Well, she's our guest, and she's bringing her grandnephew. How she managed to corral him is beyond me. Maybe she used blackmail. I happen to know that last year he got into some kind of a scrape with his car at college, and she bailed him out of it. Anyway, he's a good-looking young fellow.

"I've ordered the dinner from a restaurant. They'll be here at six, and all you have to do is put on your prettiest dress and help me into my pink lawn. Then, if you'll set the table with the spode china, we'll be ready. And get out lots of candles. It isn't a party if you don't have candles."

Bayley shook her head, dazed. Her mother had said her principal job would be to keep up with her aunt, but who would believe that one frail old lady could always stay a jump ahead of a healthy young niece? "What did you order?" she asked.

"Everything, soup to nuts, from that French place down the street."

That night when the doorbell rang, Bayley answered it. A young man stood aside to let his aunt enter. Bayley could read his brooding look exactly: "Oh help, a hen party!" His face brightened when he saw Bayley.

If Bayley had a weakness, it was for dark men. Red hair ran in the Hughes family, shading from her own fiery mop to Chip's nondescript sandy brown. Bayley had often thought that when she got married it would have to be to a dark-complexioned man. This John Morgan was a dark one all right, with laughter glinting in his brown eyes. Bayley thanked her lucky stars she had brought along her most becoming forest green dress.

Miss Georgianna Morgan and Aunt Bayley were as alike as two peas in a pod, though Miss Morgan's hair was iron gray and cut like a man's, and she taught Latin in Brentford High, whereas Aunt Bayley's white waves softly framed her face, and she taught fourth grade. Aside from these differences, they might have been twins. Georgianna Morgan had a gaiety to match Aunt Bayley's, and they fell to arguing right away, at the same time beaming proudly on their grandniece and grandnephew.

A waiter wheeled in a wagon with the dinner and stayed to serve it. The conversation never flagged, and the aunts kept the young people in gales of laughter.

When dinner was over, Miss Morgan announced, "Now, Bayley, I'm going to sit with your aunt, and John's going to take you out. Have you any money, John? I thought not. Here's ten dollars. Scoot!"

"They want to get rid of us," John grinned.

Bayley got a sweater, and soon she was riding with John in Miss Morgan's little English car. She didn't very often feel pretty, but tonight she did. Candlelight worked wonders for red hair anyway, but the real cause was the way John looked at her. He looks at me as though I was a real desirable-type woman, Bayley thought with satisfaction. He doesn't know I'm supposed to be a rough, tough tomboy.

"What would you like to do?" he asked. "I understand there's an amusement park on a lake not far from here."

"The park's fun on a warm night like this," Bayley told him.

They started for the lake, and talked about their aunts.

"They're really something special," John mused. "I suppose it seems weird that I'd come to visit an ancient relative who teaches Latin, of all things, but Aunt Georgie and I have always been buddies."

They reached the lake and wandered around beneath

the bright lights at the park. Then they rented suits and swam to the raft anchored some distance from shore.

Bayley had been hoping to meet some of her former school friends. It wouldn't have hurt her feelings to have her Brentford pals see her in the company of a present-able male like John Morgan, but she didn't happen to meet anyone she knew.

It was romantic, lying on the raft, listening to the merry-go-round music. Bayley and John got really ac-quainted. "Aunt Georgie will loan me her car at the drop of a hat," he told her. "I'll pick you up tomorrow night if you're not tied up."

Bayley agreed to the suggestion and began to forget the awe-inspiring fact that she was actually out on a date with a college sophomore. They swam back to shore and got dressed. John threw baseballs at one of the concessions, and won Bayley a large teddy bear. It was like being kids again, and gay and fun.

When they got back to town, they discovered it was midnight, and Miss Morgan had put Aunt Bayley to bed and walked home.

Aunt Bayley was awake and listening when Bayley let herself in, and Bayley sat on the bed and told her about the evening. "I'm glad I'm not such an antique I can't dredge up a young man to squire you around," her aunt said with satisfaction. "Georgie Morgan and I were hop-ing we could promote some romance. I'm glad you liked him."

"I'm glad he liked me," Bayley said. "This glamour routine is kind of out of my line."

Her aunt seemed to understand. "You'll get the hang of it," she said confidently. "I think I ought to tell you, you looked perfectly gorgeous tonight."

"Oh, come off it," Bayley scoffed. "I couldn't look gorgeous if I spent twenty-four hours a day wallowing in the stuff they sell in the fancy jars at the drug store. You can't make a glamour-puss out of a sow's ear."

"Don't you call my niece a sow's ear," Aunt Bayley ordered. "Now, go to bed."

XIII

BAYLEY HAD FUN during the rest of that week in Brentford. Her duties were light. Caring for her aunt's apartment seemed like tending a doll's house. Each day, Aunt Bayley took on more jobs, dusting and mending and helping in the kitchen. She told Bayley, "Frankly, I'm just being selfish to let your mother come back at all. I could manage alone. But I figure this way, I may never again get a chance to entice her away from your father. So I'm working this busted hip to a fare-thee-well."

She fussed like a mother hen over Bayley's casual romance with John Morgan. She insisted that her niece buy dresses Bayley didn't really need.

She explained why. "I watched you growing up, child. Your brothers swamped you. I don't know how your mother manages to hang onto her personality as a woman. Land sakes, you were just a little thing when you started having to compete with them, in order to survive.

"Now don't bristle," she said. "Your tribe is no worse than the general run of men. But us women have to stick together, and I saw the way they used to knock you

139

around. Instead of learning girlish arts and wiles, you had to learn judo, poor child!"

In one of their intimate talks, Bayley spoke about her freckles. Aunt Bayley had no panacea for them, but she said, "Don't let them bother you. They're very attractive in a homely sort of a way. However, you might try a pancake make-up and a brighter lipstick."

When Bayley dressed to go out with John, her aunt poked and twitched at her, to make sure she looked her best. "I never thought you cared a hoot about clothes and how you looked," Bayley protested.

"I didn't, and that's why I never managed to snag a husband," Aunt Bayley said.

"We always thought you stayed single because you wanted to."

"Actually, I suppose that's true. I admit I've been a little smug about my life. I had all the joys of raising your mother, and none of the disadvantages of having to cater to a husband. Lately, though, I've been kind of sorry. It seems to me your dad and mother have a perfect kind of life, or as nearly perfect as it can be in this vale of tears. I suppose if I'd married I'd be tied now to a crotchety, cantankerous old man, nursing his arthritis and putting up with his whims. But maybe it would be worth it."

Bayley was surprised to see that her aunt actually looked wistful. Aunt Bayley caught her look and laughed. "Don't pay me any mind, child. By tomorrow I'll be thanking my stars I kept my independence. I just didn't want you to think I never had any beaux. Oh, I did all right. Ask anybody in Brentford. I had lots of men dangling on my string."

A letter came from Bruno that week, beginning, "I hope you don't mind my taking the liberty of writing you," which was a pretty startling and formal attitude. Bruno told of meeting Jean, and said she wanted to go "rocking," too. They were waiting for Bayley to come home, to make the trip to the garnet pit. Bruno sounded amazed that the girls considered geology a fun sort of thing.

He added that there was real neighboring going on in the back yards between the Sudak house and the Hughes house. His father and Bayley's mother were gardening together.

One evening, John took Bayley to dance at the public pavilion at the lake. Bayley had noticed a shop on the lake road called the Pink Dinosaur, which advertised minerals and petrified wood. The shop was lit, and Bayley said on impulse, "Let's go in."

She was confused when they stepped inside. A man came forward. "May I help you?"

"I don't know," Bayley said doubtfully, looking over the displays of minerals and cases of polished slabs of stone. "I want to give somebody a present, but I don't know what."

"Who's this character you're buying a present for?" John asked.

"Oh, he's just the boy next door. I sort of owe him something, because he took me on a geology trip and I sprained my ankle and spoiled everything."

"Perhaps your friend would like some nice crystals," the clerk suggested. "Does he collect geodes?"

"I wouldn't know. What's a geode?"

"They're rather interesting. We have some from Brazil and also from Iowa."

He led the way to a display of things that looked like plain, gray stones or the petrified eggs of some prehistoric beast. They had been chiseled in two. The clerk opened several, and Bayley exclaimed. They were hollow and contained delicate white or lavender or yellow crystals. She took a long time deciding, then brought a small one which had small crystals of amethyst.

Well satisfied with her purchase, she tucked the package in her pocket. John seemed somewhat out of sorts when they started on toward the lake. "Love sends a little gift of rocks," he muttered. "What kind of a screwball is this guy?"

Some newly awakened instinct told Bayley to smile mysteriously and say nothing. Let John think this was a great romance if he wanted to.

At the pavilion, they ran into Amy, Bayley's best friend in the old days, with several other boys and girls from the old crowd at Brentford High. Bayley's girl friends had dropped in at her aunt's apartment when they learned she was back in town. Now everybody seemed pleased, but also somewhat surprised, to see Bayley with a good-looking boy like John Morgan. They insisted that the two join them at a table on the veranda overlooking the lake.

Luckily, Bayley's three brothers had taught her to be a good dancer, and she had a lovely evening.

Amy and Jimmie arranged a double date with her and John, before the party broke up.

"I hear tell there's a Lover's Lane on the other side of the lake," John suggested as they started home.

"Yes, and there's a Brentford cop who patrols it," Bayley told him.

Nevertheless, John drove around the lake and parked the car where others were stopped, and snapped off the lights. They watched the stars dancing on the black water. Bayley was flustered; her experience of this type of situation was limited. John pulled her to him and his mouth found hers. She was passive, not kissing him back. She wasn't at all sure what would happen if she did.

Her problem was solved by the appearance of Officer Donnelly, who came along the line of cars sticking his flashlight in the windows. "All right, kids," he said in a fatherly voice. "Break it up and go along home now."

Other cars started up. John grumbled, "What's the matter, does this town have a grudge against romance?" Then he took Bayley home.

The week ended all too soon. On Saturday, Bayley went to the store to do an errand for her aunt, and Benjy and her mother arrived while she was gone. Bayley opened the door, and there they were.

Her mother folded her in her arms. "My goodness, you look nice. You look really grown up! What has Aunt Bay been doing to you?"

She went on to explain, "We came a day early because Dad's company is having its annual clambake tomorrow, and he couldn't bring me. Benjy offered to drive me over today."

Aunt Bayley said crossly, "It didn't occur to either of you, did it, that you might be interfering with Bayley's love life? She had a date for tonight."

"That's all right," Bayley put in. "It wasn't anything special. I'll call John and explain."

John refused to say good-bye over the telephone, however, and insisted that Bayley wait until he could get there. It didn't hurt her feelings at all to have her twin brother find out she had acquired a boy friend as presentable as John Morgan.

He met her family and stayed to talk for a few minutes. When Bayley went to the door with him, he kissed her in front of them, and made her promise she would write.

After John had gone, all Benjy said was "Huh!"

"What do you mean, 'Huh?' " Aunt Bayley demanded.

"I didn't mean anything," Benjy mumbled. "I just meant, 'Huh.' Where'd you drag him up, Bay?"

"He's just somebody I met," Bayley said vaguely, waving her hand airily as though John Morgan were only one of dozens who had been besieging her all week.

Benjy returned to the subject when he and Bayley were driving back to Fenfield. "How about this Morgan character?" he demanded.

"What do you mean, how about him?" Bayley repressed a smile, seeing how difficult it was for her twin to accept the fact that a college man found his sister attractive.

"I mean, you're not serious about him, are you?"

"For heaven's sakes, no. We just had fun together."

Benjy was silent for a while, hunched over the wheel. Then he said, "How come you're wearing all that stuff on your fingernails?"

"Why shouldn't I wear polish on my fingernails? Everybody does."

Benjy chewed on that. Then he said, "You're not everybody."

"What do you mean, I'm not everybody?"

Benjy growled, "You're my sister."

Bayley began to get mad. "So I'm your sister. Big deal. So I have to drag around like an old sack of flour because you don't want to see me look nice. I'm just that good-natured slob Bayley, who's good enough to cook for you and sew on your darn old buttons and stuff like that, but she ought not to get any ideas that she isn't so bad-looking or anything like that! Let me tell you, brother dear, you've pushed me around long enough!"

Benjy cowered as though she were raining blows on him. "I don't know what's bugging you. I never pushed you around."

"Yes, you did. You pushed me around plenty. But you won't do it any more, hear?"

"Yes, I hear," Benjy said, "and so can anybody else within fifty miles. Stop yelling."

"I wasn't yelling."

"Yes, you *were* yelling!"

Bayley in her turn went into an ominous silence. Then she suddenly laughed. "What are we fighting about?" she asked.

A smile broke over Benjy's face. He had just about the sweetest smile in the world when he chose to use it. "I don't know," he said mildly.

That was the end of the quarrel. They had been fighting this way, fiercely and briefly, since the day they first learned to talk.

In an offhand way, Bayley mentioned what had happened when she and John had parked on Lover's Lane, the night they went dancing. "I felt like a sap," she said. "Here I am, at my advanced age, and I'm still so dumb about boys I actually got scared. I wanted to kiss him back, but I didn't."

"I'm glad you're that kind of dumb," Benjy muttered.

"Yes, but if you were out with a girl you wouldn't want her to act so stupid."

"That's different."

"What's different?"

"You're my sister."

Here it was again. In Benjy's opinion and in Tom's and even in Chip's, Bayley guessed, a sister was in an entirely different category from other girls. Her brothers couldn't be argued out of this belief.

She dropped the subject and asked about affairs at home. Benjy gave her what little news had accumulated in the week she had been away. "Your other boy friend was over," he said. "Bruno, the long drink of water."

Bayley fired up again. "Listen, just because he likes me you don't have to make fun of him."

"I wasn't making fun of him. Take that chip off your shoulder, Bay. Dr. Sudak was over, too, and he and Dad and Mother got to be real pals. And Saja came over." He stopped.

"What about Saja?" Bayley prompted him.

"Oh, nothing." Benjy went on again after a moment, bursting out with "Boy, is that girl bright!"

"There's no law that says a girl can't have brains," Bayley informed him.

"I know it, I know it, and on her they look good."

"Did Mother ever meet Mrs. Sudak?"

"No," Benjy said, "I don't believe she did."

XIV

IT WAS VERY PLEASANT to be home again. Of course, her mother had left everything in apple-pie order, and that made housekeeping easier. It was really quite flattering, in an exasperating sort of way, to have the whole load of the complicated household dumped on her and to be expected to cope competently. She realized for the first time, when she found herself automatically performing the hundred and one different chores, how much she had learned about her job.

Naturally, wild horses wouldn't have dragged any such admission from her brothers. Chip made the obvious crack, "Ugh, back to the slops again," when they sat down to their first Bayley-cooked meal.

Mr. Hughes glowered at his youngest and growled, "Lay off your sister. Your mother never made a better stew than this."

Bruno Sudak came across the lawns to look at Mrs. Hughes's roses. At least, that was his excuse. He was so diffident and funny he still didn't pop over or barge into the house whenever he felt like it. No, he still thought he had to invent a reason. "I came to find out when you would like to go to the garnet pit, Bayley."

"Any day," she told him. "How about Jean? Didn't you say she wanted to go?"

"Yes, and your brother expressed an interest."

"Which brother?"

"Your twin."

"Benjy?" Bayley exclaimed, disbelieving. Benjy had been the principal scoffer when Bayley first developed an interest in rocks.

She knew he was in the garage polishing his beloved, beat-up car, and she called, "Benjy, do you want to go rocking with us?"

He came out, wiping his hands on an old cloth. "Okay, I don't mind."

"You don't have to go if you don't want to."

"How about Saja?" Benjy asked.

"What about Saja?" questioned Bayley.

"Is she going, too?"

Bruno allowed that she probably might.

"I'll call Jean now," Bayley suggested. "Let's do it tomorrow. That's Benjy's day off."

She was thoroughly confused. Which girl was Benjy planning to date on this expedition, Jean or Saja?

Bruno stood up as though he was preparing to flee, and Bayley ordered, "You stay right there. I've got something for you."

She called Jean, but it turned out that Jean had a steady baby-sitting job every day that week, and she told Bayley,

"You go this time without me, and if it turns out to be fun then I can go next time."

Bayley ran upstairs to fetch the gift she had brought for Bruno. He recognized what it was immediately when he unwrapped it. "A geode!"

"I suppose you've got a million of them."

"No, I don't own one. There's a good collection in the geology lab. I say, Bayley, I'm really delighted!"

Benjy sauntered over to see what was interesting them. Bruno explained how, eons ago, the strange hollow rock had been formed, with the amethyst inside crystallized in delicate lavender.

Benjy was impressed. "Maybe there's something to this geology racket after all," he admitted. "Now, that's a fairly interesting object."

Bruno was overwhelmed by his gift. In fact, he was quite incoherent as he tried to express his thanks.

"Ye gods, it's only a rock," Bayley protested, "but I'm glad you like it."

He carefully put the two parts together and bore it home as proudly as though Bayley had endowed him with a priceless relic.

Saja emerged from the Sudak house shortly after and stopped to talk a minute. Bayley was delighted to see how young she looked, in the shorts and blouse that were practically a summer uniform, that would make her blend into any crowd of her contemporaries. Yet how distinguished she looked, with dark serious eyes in a narrow face! Her high-bridged nose gave her a patrician air.

Bayley instinctively felt her own nose. It seemed like a blob, serviceable but not decorative.

"Why don't we take a picnic tomorrow?" Bayley suggested to Saja, who nodded in agreement. "I'll make things and you make things, and we've got a Thermos bucket for ice, and the boys can get soda."

The next morning, Benjy fussed around the kitchen, critically watching his sister putting sandwiches together. Bayley got the impression that the lunch was important principally because Saja was going.

Jerry happened to drop in. This was the first time Bayley had seen him since she had turned down the date to play tennis. "Picnic," he observed. "Where to?"

"We're going rocking," Bayley told him. "Don't you want to come along?"

"I'm afraid the geology bit is a little out of my line," he said. "How come you've developed such a burning thirst for nature lore, Benjy?"

"I just thought I'd give it a whirl," Benjy said vaguely. "I'm suspending judgment until I see what it's like."

"It's fun in a grubby kind of way," Bayley told them, "but it can be hard work, too, if it's a hot day. If you want to change your mind, Jerry, say the word and I'll make a couple of extra sandwiches."

"No, I'll wait for Benjy's report," Jerry went on, "There's a good picture at the Bijou Friday night. Either of you want to go?"

"I've got a date," Benjy said.

"How about you, Bay?"

"I guess so." It was such a lukewarm invitation, it called for a lukewarm answer.

"I'll pick you up at seven."

He evidently didn't recognize the new, glamorous Bayley who had emerged during the week she had spent in Brentford. After she got home, Bayley had enjoyed forgetting she was that suave, soigné type and getting back into comfortable dungarees. Now she thought to herself, Tactical error, old girl. He still thinks he's dealing with the uncouth character he used to know.

She gave him her most radiant smile and said, "Seven's fine. I'll be ready."

When Benjy parked in front of the Sudak house and leaned on the horn, Bruno was startled. He came out, bearing his sister's contribution to the feast, and asked, "Aren't we going to walk?"

"How far is it?" Benjy asked.

"Five miles south of town, on Route 142."

"Are you nuts?" Benjy demanded, shocked at the suggestion. "Hop in."

Bayley was in the back seat. She noticed that Saja waited for her brother to open the door for her so she could sit in front beside Benjy, and Bayley made a mental note. That's where these European girls have got it all over us. They expect men to be courteous. We don't give American men a chance to be polite. If I waited that way for Benjy to open a door, he'd only say, "What's the matter, are you a cripple or something?"

"What's the bag for?" she asked Bruno. "I guess I can put all the garnets I'll find in my pockets."

"We might find other specimens," he told her. He rummaged in his rucksack. "This is a present for you." He brought out a short-handled hammer with a pick on one end.

Bayley caught her twin's grin. Well, maybe this did seem a funny present to give a girl, but she was really thrilled. She hefted it. "Thanks, Bruno. I feel like an honest-to-goodness prospector now."

"I hope somebody brought along some bandages to hold Bay together in case she takes any more falls," Benjy commented.

The Sudaks still didn't seem to understand the kidding that was as natural as breathing to everybody in the Hughes family. Bayley let Benjy's remark die a natural death without retorting.

Finding their way by Bruno's map, they turned off Route 142 and entered deep woods, through an overgrown lane which was little better than a wood road. Benjy recognized the foolishness of taking the car farther and backed it into the bushes, out of the way of other cars. "It doesn't look as though anybody has been through here in years, though," he pointed out. They loaded up and started walking.

The fragrant hemlock woods were absolutely still, except for bird talk, which seemed unnaturally loud. Benjy laughed because he caught himself tiptoeing. "It's my Boy Scout training," he explained.

Bayley was amused to see how he imitated the way Bruno was helping her over the fallen tree trunks. Each time, Benjy carefully took Saja's elbow. Bayley thought again, If he and I were alone, he'd only get impatient while I scrambled over by myself. This trip is doing Benjy a lot of good. He's finding out that having good manners isn't necessarily a sign of mental and moral decay.

Bruno pointed ahead. "That must be the sand bank." The wood road skirted a high mound of sand, which obviously had been excavated by heavy machinery.

They set the lunch under a tree on thick, soft moss. Bruno began turning over stones with his foot. Then he stooped. "The first garnet is for Bayley."

The one he gave her was massive, measuring an inch in diameter. "Its facets are almost perfect," he explained, turning it for them to see.

"I thought garnets were red stones they made jewelry of," Benjy said, confused by the others' enthusiasm for this muddy-brown object.

"I doubt we'll find gem garnet, but we may," Bruno told him. "These are industrial garnets. They probably excavated this area to mine them for abrasives to make emery paper." He launched into an explanation of how the formation had evolved in ages past. Benjy looked harassed, the way he always did when somebody tried to force a little learning on him.

Saja had started to climb the mound, the sand slipping away under her feet. Benjy, relieved to get away from the more earnest geologists of the party, scrambled after her, and the two disappeared from sight.

Bayley and Bruno worked together until they had collected an impressive number of stones. Bayley's dungaree

154

pockets were sagging. Bruno gathered the more perfect specimens, trying to find many of the same size, about a half-inch in diameter. Finally he volunteered the reason. "I'm going to make you a necklace," he confided. "It won't be very handsome, but nobody else will have one like it."

"How are you going to do that?"

"I've got a tumbler rigged up in our cellar. Haven't you heard it?"

"Is that the low, rumbling noise we hear coming out of your house?"

"Yes. I've invented a polishing machine. I bought a quarter-horsepower motor which turns two parallel rollers. I seal the stones in a coffee can, with water and abrasive, and put the can on the rollers, and the stones tumble around and polish themselves. I saw a picture of such a machine in one of your wonderful American magazines on mechanics."

"Good grief," Bayley exclaimed, "if Benjy and Chip had known anything like that was going on in your cellar, they'd have been over there as fast as though they'd been shot out of a gun! They drool over any kind of a machine."

"The garnets will lose their facets when they are tumbled, but I think they'll make an interesting necklace."

Saja was calling from the top of the hill, "Come up here! It's very interesting."

Bruno and Bayley gathered up the picnic and climbed the sandy mound. They found the other two comfortably sitting on a log, sifting sand with their fingers, finding loose garnets of a better cut than those which had washed down the hill.

A wire fence bore a sign, "Admission one dollar. Inquire at farmhouse." They were discussing whether it would be worth the dollar to try exploring the restricted area for better stones, when a collie dog came sniffing along, followed by a man. "What'll we find if we pay the dollar?" Benjy sang out.

The man leaned on a fence post and solemnly regarded them. "Well, I could take your money and tell you you'd pick up a fortune in gems," he said, "but I won't. It's been years since anybody has unearthed any worthwhile stones. I keep the sign up to discourage people from crossing my land and leaving the bars down and letting my cows out. You can come through the fence for free if you'll be careful about putting back the bars. If you want water to drink, you can come to the house and dip out of my well."

They thanked him and watched him out of sight. The collie, after sniffing them all and saying hello with his wagging tail, followed his master.

"He didn't carry a gun," Saja said.

Benjy looked at her, startled. "Why should he?"

"This is a lonely place. I think he should carry a gun for protection."

Bayley, too, was puzzled. "Why should he need a gun? He's just a nice farmer."

"Somebody might rob him."

"He probably hasn't got anything worth stealing,"

Benjy said. "I guess you've been seeing too many western movies. Things like that don't happen in real life."

Saja asked, "In this country do people walk on other people's land when they wish?"

"Sure, unless there's a sign that says specifically not to. It's a big country. Why should anyone mind people walking on his land?"

Saja persisted, "If we had disregarded the sign and crossed his fence without permission, would he have called the police?"

Benjy frowned, trying to understand what was behind Saja's questions. He said, "If he was a crank or nut or something, he might. But this man wouldn't. If the police came, they'd only find us, and what harm are we doing? As long as a person isn't doing any damage, he's free to do just about anything he likes."

"I've seen many signs along the roads around Fenfield," Saja pointed out. "They say, 'Keep Out. No Trespassing.'"

"That's different," Benjy told her. "The signs also probably said, 'No Hunting or Fishing.' Lots of people post their land to keep hunters out. There's a hunting season in the fall when it's legal to shoot pheasants and other birds, and small game. Most people post their land because they don't want animals or birds killed, but nobody in his right mind would try to have people arrested when they're just out in the country for a walk."

"You lived in England," Bayley said. "In England

157

they didn't threaten you with guns when you went for country walks, did they?"

"We lived in London," Bruno told her. "We didn't get out in the country."

Saja's face had cleared, and she said, "Thank you. There are many things I do not understand, and the only way I can learn is by asking questions."

"Ask away," Benjy said gallantly.

They spread the tablecloth on pine needles and lounged in the cool shade to eat their lunch. Benjy was enlightening Saja about high school and what she should expect, telling her about the point system and extracurricular activities and sports. Bayley was startled to hear him promising to help Saja with math, since she planned to take advanced algebra. It was on the tip of Bayley's tongue to say, "That'll be the day! Talk about the blind leading the blind."

She stopped in time. Then she tried to puzzle out in her own mind why she had stopped. Why did the Sudak twins inhibit her from making any crack she pleased about her brother's lack of brains? Why were both she and Benjy leaning over backwards to be polite today, even to each other?

Not that it was such a strain, Bayley realized. It was almost as easy to be courteous to Benjy as it was to snarl at him.

She wondered if he, too, realized how strangely they were behaving. She rather thought he did. The sandwich basket was on his and Saja's side, and Benjy asked,

"Would you like another sandwich, Sis?" Then he flushed. Ordinarily, it wouldn't have occurred to him to notice that his sister's plate was empty, or if it had he might have said, "Hey, Dopey, want a sandwich?"

She told Benjy about the machine Bruno had rigged for polishing stones, and, as she had expected, Benjy reacted enthusiastically. "I want to see that. I'll be over."

She caught the startled look that flashed between Saja and Bruno. They weren't ready yet, she saw, to accept fully a free and easy neighborliness. Their mother's illness prevented that.

The four explored the ravine on the other side of the hill. Bayley trailed Bruno, tapping at rocks, proudly using the new pick he had given her.

Although he was loaded with equipment, he managed to take her hand to help her as they made their way back to the car. Saja and Benjy dawdled behind, still turning over gravel looking for treasures. Bruno suddenly put his arm around Bayley and pulled her hard against him. "I like you so much, Bayley."

"Well, thanks. I like you, too." It seemed an inadequate sort of response, but it satisfied him. All the way home in the car, Bruno kept tight hold of her hand.

XV

A LETTER CAME from Mrs. Hughes that week. "I'm coming home to stay a week from Saturday," she wrote. "Your Aunt Bayley is a spoiled old woman and she's just using me for a good thing. She's a nosy old woman, too. She's reading this over my shoulder.

"I remember now that when I was home I mixed up Tom's and Benjy's socks. Boys, please switch them back.

"I didn't do anything about Mrs. Sudak, either, because I didn't want to force the issue. When I'm home to stay, you and I will talk that matter over, Bayley."

She went on with a full page of instructions for the care and feeding of her precious garden during the hot August days.

What happened soon after, on a calm, sunny morning, just went to prove that neighborliness is a good thing even if it borders on nosiness. In other words, people ought to keep close tabs on people who live nearby.

Bayley and Chip were working together in the kitchen, trying to figure out what ailed the vacuum cleaner, which was in a growling mood. If Bayley had given the Sudak family a thought, she would have vaguely realized that

Bruno was probably at the university, where he was help-ing make a contour map in the geography department, that as usual, Dr. Sudak was in his chemistry lab at Fallon Hall and Saja was helping him.

Bayley wasn't thinking, however; she was only con-cerned that Chip put back the right number of vacuum-cleaner parts in the right order. She became aware that Happy was barking in the back yard.

The barks grew more insistent, and Bayley said, "I don't care if Happy's talking to the moles under the lawn, but if he's digging holes in Mother's rose border we'll have to teach him a lesson. Go and see, Chip."

"Go and see yourself," Chip retorted automatically.

"No, you go," Bayley ordered. Until her mother came home she was still boss, and she intended to hang on to her authority until the last possible moment.

"Okay," Chip grumbled. The minute he stepped out-side, he yelled, "Bay, come on!"

Smoke was pouring out the Sudaks' back door, eddy-ing up through the trees. Through the window, Bayley caught a glimpse of a dull, red glow.

"Call the fire department!" Chip bellowed, and Bayley didn't stop to argue, but did as she was told.

When she came out again, Chip was desperately wres-tling to open the Sudaks' back door. Bayley knew it was kept locked when Mrs. Sudak was home alone, and she yelled, "Let's try to get in through the cellar!" Just then, Chip threw his weight against the door and fell inside. Bayley followed.

The acrid smell of burning grease almost drove her back, but she seized a towel and held it to her face. The red glow came from the stove. When fresh air blew in, the smoldering fire burst into bright flame. The wooden cupboards over the stove caught fire, and flames licked up along the curtains to the ceiling.

Chip was like a dynamo. He snatched up the table-cloth, and, using it to protect his hands, he seized the blazing pan and threw it out the door. Choking and sput-tering, he rummaged under the sink and found a kettle, filled it with water, and started dousing the blazing woodwork and walls. Bayley watched in dumb admira-tion. He hadn't hesitated; he had known instantly what to do and had gone ahead and done it.

Then Bayley thought of Mrs. Sudak! She must be somewhere in the house. Calling as she went, Bayley stumbled through the smoke-filled rooms. She started up the stairs.

Up there, the smoke wasn't so bad. All the hall doors were shut. She opened one after another, crying, "Mrs. Sudak, please answer me!" The rooms were neat and empty.

Bayley paused, listening. Chip was banging around downstairs, but up here there was silence. She heard a sound coming from behind a closed door, a sound that could only be a muffled sob. She crossed the hall and threw open the door, disclosing an old-fashioned bathroom.

Mrs. Sudak was standing there, her hands over her face. Bayley gently led her out of the bathroom and into the master bedroom, murmuring, "Everything's all right. My brother is putting out the fire. There's nothing to be afraid of."

The older woman didn't try to shrink away. She trembled, and Bayley put her arms around her, trying to give her a feeling of safety.

With a horrible shrieking, the fire engine roared up and stopped with a squealing of tires in front of the house. Bayley heard men shouting, trampling through the rooms. She longed to go and see what was happening, but, when she tried to loosen her arms, Mrs. Sudak tightened her hold. "It's all right," Bayley soothed her. "I won't leave you."

She began smoothing the gray hair away from Mrs. Sudak's face. She was amazed and touched to find that this gentle gesture quieted her fear.

Feet pounded on the stairs, and Chip appeared, his face black and sweating, an apparition that would have frightened anyone. "You all right?" he asked. "The fire's out. I had it under control before the firemen got here. What happened, Mrs. Sudak? The chief wants to know."

Mrs. Sudak only hid her face in Bayley's shoulder. "Go away," Bayley ordered. "You're scaring her even more."

"Yeah, but he has to find out what started the fire. There's not much damage, but they have to know."

"It's as plain as the nose on your face," Bayley said. "She was cooking, and the pan of grease caught fire. Get them out of the house as soon as you can, Chip. She's nervous, and the way they're yelling and banging makes her worse. Tell them she's sick and can't come down."

"Okay." Chip vanished.

Bayley heard the firemen gathering up their hoses. The smoke had cleared entirely from this upstairs room.

The next feet on the stairs were quiet ones. Dr. Sudak looked in, his face pale with concern for his wife. "Bayley, I'm so glad you're here. How is she?"

"She's all right. She's had an awful fright, but she's calming down now."

"Your brother was wonderful. He was complete master of the situation."

His wife obediently swallowed the pills he gave her. His children came in, and the doctor told Saja, "Your mother will be tranquil now. Help her to bed." With an admiring look for Bayley, Bruno left the room. Saja began loosening her mother's dress, murmuring soothingly.

It was difficult, because Mrs. Sudak wouldn't release Bayley's hand. Bayley helped put her into a cotton wrapper. "She has a real feeling for you, Bayley," Saja said. "Since the day you came and brought the gift of the cake, she has watched you from the windows. If we hear her laughing, we know you are in your yard playing with your dog. When you go along the street, she watches you out of sight. It has become a family joke that Mama likes you better than she does us."

Bayley didn't answer, because tears pressed against her eyelids. Mrs. Sudak lay back against the pillow, her eyes closed, but her thin fingers still clung to Bayley's. Finally

Bayley asked, "Why didn't you tell me? I would have loved to come over and visit with her."

"A young girl should not have to concern herself with a sick woman," Saja said haltingly.

"But that's crazy! We're neighbors!"

Saja said, "Bayley, you truly believe that we all are our brother's keepers."

"I never thought about that," Bayley told her. "We're neighbors, that's all. And I like your mother. I think she's dear and sweet, and if she's scared that's not her fault, it's because she went through such terrible things years ago. My mother is coming home soon to stay, and then your mother will have a woman her own age for a friend, and that will do her a world of good."

"I doubt your mother can do more for Mama than you have already. See, she is sleeping now. We can leave her."

They went down. Bruno and his father were surveying the ruined kitchen while Chip explained what had happened. "But why didn't she just take the pan off the plate when it caught fire?" he asked.

"She probably ran in panic," the doctor said. He drew Bayley to him and kissed her on the forehead to show his gratitude.

Bruno was pulling down the charred wood. "I didn't let the firemen use water," Chip said. "Sometimes that does more damage than fire. This isn't so bad. I'll help you clean it up, Bruno."

That evening at dinner, the fire was the chief topic

of conversation, of course. Chip modestly let his sister tell how well he had coped with the crisis, how he had actually put the fire out before the firemen arrived. The family looked at the youngest with new eyes. He had showed real courage and resourcefulness.

Afterward, while Bayley was waiting for Jerry to come to take her to the movies, Tom sniffed as she passed by him. "You still smell smoky," he remarked.

Jerry spoke of it, too. Bayley had gone back to her room and liberally doused herself with a spicy scent, but Jerry asked, "How come you smell as though you'd been in a fire?"

"I was," she said. "Oh, dear, I bathed, but I didn't have time to wash my hair." She told him what had happened next door.

Jerry sounded disgruntled. "You seem to like that Polish family a lot better than you do your old friends."

Bayley looked at him in amazement. Did Jerry really count himself an old friend? Actually, this was the first time he had taken her out on an honest-to-goodness date. "Oh, well," she said lightly, "hands across the sea and all that."

"Even old Benjy acts like an egghead since he started going with Saja. She's got too much of the gray matter in the upper story to suit my taste."

"I suppose you think you don't have that problem with me."

"At least, it doesn't show on you," Jerry assured her. "It's my opinion that she and her brother spell trouble

166

with a capital T for our class next year. There's nothing that disrupts a school like a couple of real bright kids. They spoil the teachers and give them ideas about setting high standards and flunking the rest of us."

Jerry soon forgot his grievances, however, and turned out to be a good date. The week Bayley had spent going out with John Morgan in Brentford had given her a new confidence. If you could handle a college sophomore, she realized, you had no trouble managing somebody like Jerry. She wondered now why she had felt so clumsy and tongue-tied when she first came to Fenfield, why she had worried so much about joining the high-school gang.

After the movie, Jerry drove to the Kampus Kitchen, where a dozen of the boys and girls of their class were congregated. Somebody said, "Hi, Bayley, where have you been keeping yourself all summer?"

Jean joined them, with Andy Phelps. Jean had given Benjy up as a bad job, but that hadn't spoiled her friendship with Bayley.

They were pushing two tables together when somebody asked, "How about going to the river for a swim?" They scattered in various cars to collect swimsuits.

"I've got a suit you can borrow," Bayley told Jean, so the four went in Jerry's car.

The air was cool, with a feel of autumn in it, but the river was warm. Bayley had a sudden feeling of nostalgia as she swam with lazy strokes across to the opposite bank and turned back again. She was remembering a night like this when it had been John swimming beside her.

She had had only one letter from him. I guess he didn't look on ours as a soul-searing love affair, she decided.

"You're awfully quiet tonight," Jean mentioned, while they splashed their feet from the dock, to scatter the star reflections.

"Am I?" Bayley had been pursuing a line of thought, looking back over the summer weeks, seeing how one thing had led to another. She didn't feel like the same person she had been in June. It's been a pretty good summer, she thought. I've learned a lot, and most of it has been good.

"Phew! Somebody on this dock smells like a wet dog!" one of the boys exclaimed.

Bayley laughed and admitted, "I guess it's me. I was in a fire today."

She told them about it, and they all fell to speculating about the Sudak twins. Jerry repeated his foreboding that Bruno and Saja spelled trouble. "Think what they'll do to our average," he gloomed.

Somebody remarked that Benjy didn't seem exactly intimidated because Saja was the intellectual type. Jean warmed Bayley's heart by announcing firmly, "I know her, and she's a nice kid, and none of us is doing them any great favor by treating them decently, believe me. It won't do us any permanent damage to have a couple of high I.Q.'s in the class."

Bayley knew now that Saja and Bruno would have a minimum of trouble when they started school. It could have been really rough, she realized. Their clothes, their old-world manners, their precise speech, and most of all their superior preparation could have made them seem like oddballs. Now, at least, they had the boys and girls of their class interested and curious about getting to know them, and ready to be friendly. She and Jean and Benjy had accomplished that much.

On the way back to town, naturally Jerry wanted to park, but his was an amateurish performance. Bayley was surprised how meekly he took it when she moved away from him and ordered, "Come on, I want to go home."

Once, she would have been afraid that, if she refused Jerry, he would command, "Go and never get in my convertible again." Tonight, he didn't leave until she had agreed to a date for doubles with Jean and Andy at the school tennis courts the next afternoon.

Mr. Hughes was dozing in his chair in the living room, with the late, late show on. He followed her to the kitchen when she went to get a glass of milk. "Did you have a nice evening, kitten? I guess I ought to play the heavy parent. Tom was upset when he got in at twelve and you weren't home yet. Thank heavens, your mother will be back next week, to lay down the rules. I'm not sure whether I'm supposed to be irate or not. After all, it's after one."

"No, you're not supposed to be mad," Bayley assured him. "Believe me, Pops, it was just an ordinary evening. Look, here's the note I left for you, under the sugar bowl.

I came home after the movies to collect my bathing suit. I suppose you were out bowling with some of your pals from your office."

"I didn't see the note, but that's all right. I know you can take care of yourself.

"Look, kitten," he went on, while they companionably divided what was left of a chocolate cake, "you're so popular even your old man has to make a date with you in advance. Don't plan anything for this Friday night. Okay?"

"Okay, Dad. Where'd you get the idea I was as popular as all that, though? What's going on Friday night?"

"Never mind," her father said vaguely. "Just hold yourself available. That's all I can tell you."

"And the next day we'll go to Brentford, and Mother will come home for good."

"For good is right."

"Oh, now, come off it," Bayley scoffed. "I don't notice that you've exactly withered away or gone into a decline under my care, any more than your sons have."

XVI

It was a contented sort of week. As a matter of fact, it was an idyllic week, this last one that Bayley was responsible for the running of the house and the well-being of its inhabitants.

Everything seemed to go well. Happy had resigned himself to life on the end of a rope and no longer chafed against his fate. The laundry got done promptly. The vacuum cleaner had no more temper tantrums. The house had the serene, welcoming air that resulted from good care.

Also, the house was quieter. Chip's jazz combo had broken up when good old Charlie sold his trumpet to get the money to take a correspondence course in radio repairing.

Tom, Benjy, and Chip ate the meals Bayley set before them, and if they did not compliment her that was only because they were afraid of spoiling her. If Tom was careless with cigarette ashes, he brushed up the mess himself. She didn't have to yap at him. He just naturally wanted to be helpful.

Mrs. Hughes' roses had taken a new lease on life and

were blooming like crazy, as though they, too, were getting ready for their mistress' return. "That's powerful stuff Dr. Sudak put on them," Tom commented. "Let's put some on your hair, Runt, and see if it'll make that grow." He twined his fingers in Bayley's russet mop.

As a matter of fact, Bayley had become so efficient at her job, she found she actually had free hours in the afternoon, when her little world was under control and no chores nagged at her conscience. Saja often came over for female talk. Bruno crossed the lawns to inquire formally, "May I sit with you?" and to show her new mineral samples he had acquired.

He took it for granted she, too, was really wrapped up in the "geology bit." Bayley didn't have the heart to break the news to him that, while she liked collecting rocks as a hobby, she didn't look on it as an all-absorbing career.

Bruno seemed stupefied when she gently refused to go on a rock-hunting expedition because she had a tennis date with Jerry. "A sound mind in a sound body, that's my motto," she said. "I've got to develop the old forearm."

Any kind of kidding still puzzled him. On the few occasions when he had witnessed real battles between Bayley and her brothers, his concerned face showed he really believed they were locked in mortal combat.

Bayley was sitting on the wooden bench under the willow one afternoon, vaguely thinking about the people next door. We ought to take down the privet hedge, she thought. It's a ratty-looking thing, anyway. Maybe the world would be a nicer place if everybody took down the hedges.

She became aware she was being watched, and glanced over at the next house. Mrs. Sudak was at the kitchen window. Bayley crossed the lawn, smiling, hoping her friend would not retreat to some other part of the house where Bayley would hesitate to follow.

The screen door was hooked. "Mrs. Sudak," Bayley said softly, "please open the door."

A rustle in the kitchen told her she was still there. "Mrs. Sudak, you're not afraid of me. Please unhook the door. I want to talk to you."

Mrs. Sudak, her gray hair awry, wearing her usual black, shapeless dress, came slowly to the door. She stood for a long time, staring out. Bayley gave her her most winning smile. "Please open the door."

Her eyes intent on Bayley's face, Mrs. Sudak lifted the hook and let it drop. Bayley gently pushed the door open. She had a feeling that Mrs. Sudak's mind was telling her, "Run, run!" Bayley took her hand and slowly drew her out of doors, into the yard.

She could feel the trembling of the thin body. "Now we're going to walk over to my house," Bayley said. Ever so slowly, she led Mrs. Sudak across the lawn. Mrs. Sudak continued to tremble, but her eyes, watching Bayley's face, were hopeful, trustful.

Bayley seated her on the bench under the willow, keeping up a steady, soothing conversation. "There! Now you've come to visit me, and we'll just sit here where it's cool and quiet, and you don't have to talk or anything like that, so please don't try to run away." Bayley felt in her own pocket and found her comb and started tidying the gray mass of hair. This was usually Saja's task, she knew, and now she tried to arrange the hair as Saja did.

The touch of her hands calmed Mrs. Sudak's fears better than anything else could, and Bayley kept up the combing and fussing for a long time. Then she sat with her friend in companionable silence.

Finally she said, "Mrs. Sudak, you're going to sit here all by yourself for a little while, and I'm going to the house and make us a little party." She started to move away.

With a startled cry, Mrs. Sudak arose, looking about wildly, ready to run. Bayley came back and gently pressed her down on the bench. "You're going to sit right here." Whether Mrs. Sudak understood the English words, she didn't know.

Bayley had an inspiration, and put the book she had been reading and the comb in Mrs. Sudak's lap. For some reason Mrs. Sudak understood this. She held Bayley's possessions and watched her walk up the path to the house.

Bayley poured iced tea and put cookies on a plate. She happened to glance out the window, and exclaimed, "Oh, dear, he'll ruin everything!" Happy had awakened and emerged from his cave under the rhododendrons and was bouncing across the yard to meet the stranger.

Mrs. Sudak put her hand on his head. Happy had a

bad habit of jumping on people in his exuberance, and he was quite capable of knocking them over, for he was a solid, heavy dog. Bayley fully expected him to throw his bulk on Mrs. Sudak and knock her off the bench.

But no, Happy stood still. Bayley saw her guest's fingers playing around his ridiculously long ears. It was rather like a miracle that the basset hound, who wasn't supposed to have a brain in his head, understood instantly that he must be docile. Nobody will ever tell me again he's stupid, Bayley thought, proud and gratified.

Indeed, Happy accomplished what Bayley had not been able to. A shy smile played around Mrs. Sudak's mouth.

Bayley set the tray on the table. Usually, Happy went into ecstasies at sight of food. This time he sat up expectantly, but he did not lunge at the plate, to gobble its contents in one mighty mouthful.

Mrs. Sudak sipped her tea, nibbled a cookie. She seemed to be struggling for words, and frowned. Bayley had another inspiration. "Dog," she said, breaking a tidbit for Happy. "Nice dog."

"Nice dog," Mrs. Sudak repeated.

"Happy. His name is Happy."

"Happy dog."

"Yes," Bayley said, "Happy dog."

She was thinking: Oh, if only somebody would come now and see us, because they'll never believe I managed to lure her over and that we had a party.

She heard a car stop in front of the Sudaks' house, but

it was out of sight of the hiding place under the willows. She heard Saja's musical voice calling, "Mama?" Then Saja said in a low voice, "Father, look over there."

Mrs. Sudak was absorbed in dropping bits of cookie in Happy's waiting mouth, and didn't see her husband and daughter soundlessly approaching. Bayley put her hand on her friend's arm, to quiet her in case she was startled. "We're having a party together," she said in a matter-of-fact voice. "We're having a nice party, Mrs. Sudak and Bayley and Happy dog."

Mrs. Sudak looked up and saw her husband, and now her smile was radiant, illuminating her worn face. "Happy dog," she said loudly.

They stayed under the willow, talking together, until Bruno joined them, and then the whole family walked home. Bayley caught a shine of tears behind the doctor's thick glasses as he said, "What we prayed for has happened. Now that the wall she built around herself has been breached, I think she will venture out into the world."

Bayley told her own family about it that evening. "You're kidding," Benjy said. "You got her out of the house?"

"Yes, and you should have seen Happy. Nobody'll ever call him stupid again while I'm around. That dog knows a heck of a lot about psychology. I didn't have to tell him to behave. He naturally did the right thing."

She went on, "I got to thinking today, we ought to

176

take down the hedge between us and the house next door."

"Why?" Tom asked.

"Well, it's a scrubby sort of a thing, and I don't like hedges and fences. They keep people out. Or they keep people in."

Bayley was talking idly, but her father bent a serious look on her. "I don't believe hedges or fences will ever bother you much, daughter," he said. "You'll find a way over or through or around them somehow."

That week was such a busy one, Bayley forgot her father's warning about saving an evening for him. He reminded her at breakfast on Friday. "Don't forget, we've got a date tonight. Wear that yellow dress you got this summer, will you? I'll be home at six."

"Okay, Dad. I'll fix dinner to leave for the boys."

"No, they're coming with us."

"That's nice, although I thought we were going to be an exclusive little twosome," Bayley said.

"No such luck. They're in on the planning, too."

There seemed to be an air of mystery in the house when the boys gathered in late afternoon. Tom came home from work promptly, instead of taking a detour to get a look at his adored Beth. Bayley couldn't help but be flattered that he was giving up a whole evening for a mere sister.

She found Benjy rummaging in their mother's clothes closet and demanded, "What are you doing in Mother's stuff?"

"None of your business," he told her.

She actually heard Chip inquire plaintively, "Tom, do you think I ought to take a bath?" Chip's suggesting such a thing was so world-shaking that Bayley couldn't believe her ears.

"Yes, of course you've got to take a bath, but let me go first. I don't want to have to scrub out the alluvial deposit you always leave in the tub."

Was everybody bathing? Bayley wondered. Chip's "Ye gods, old Bayley isn't worth it," was reassuring. At least, her entire family hadn't turned angelic and cleanly beyond all recognition.

The bathroom got a real workout, but was cleared before Mr. Hughes arrived. When he had dressed, he found his sons lined up in the living room, all immaculate, all wearing ties with their sports jackets. Bayley, in her pale yellow silk, was growing more apprehensive by the minute. All she could say as she surveyed them was, "You all look as though you were coming to my wake or something."

"Got the you know what?" her father inquired.

The "you know what" turned out to be a corsage of camellias. As Bayley wonderingly pinned it to her dress, Chip announced, "Nutsy Bayley's so nosy I had to hide it in the furnace all day."

"Stow the 'Nutsy Bayley' for tonight," Tom commanded.

Bayley looked at all her men, waiting for her gratitude. She kissed them all. The flowers were such a sudden, sweet gift that her eyes filled up.

This peculiar solicitousness continued. Instead of piling into the station wagon ahead of her, they stood back while their father gallantly helped her in. "Where are we going?" she asked.

Her father said casually, "I thought we might try the White Fox Inn. We haven't been there lately."

"We've never been there!" Bayley exclaimed. The place he named was just about the most expensive inn for miles around, and anybody who had the good luck to be taken there talked about it for months afterward.

"Haven't we? Then it's high time we went," Mr. Hughes answered.

Bayley gave a wriggle of pure pleasure. She was gladder than ever that they were all dressed to the nines. She glanced at Tom, then at her father and Chip and Benjy in the back seat. A handsomer bunch of males would be hard to assemble, she realized.

Without thinking, she reached up and turned the rear-view mirror so she could see how her camellias looked. Tom didn't even snarl at her. He simply turned it back so he could see the road behind.

This unnatural politeness was becoming painful. Bayley tried to think of some quip which would ease the tension. When she murmured some inanity, the men simply stared at her, and nobody cracked a smile.

They turned off the main road and entered a long drive to the inn. Tom drew up before the gray, chateau-like building, and a doorman took the car.

The headwaiter met them and asked them to sit in the

grand foyer, while their table was prepared. Bayley sank into a soft chair, trying to take everything in so she wouldn't omit any important detail when she gave an account of this evening to Jean. Tom said abruptly, "Your neck looks kind of naked, Sis."

Her hand went to it. She thought her string of pearls had broken without her knowing it, but it was there.

"I mean, you need something more to go with that dress." Tom thrust a long, narrow box at her.

Inside was a thin gold chain, and on it was suspended a polished piece of amethyst in a kind of gold cage. It was a delicate, lovely thing, and Bayley's throat suddenly felt lumpy. This evening was turning into a really emotional occasion. "It's beautiful. I don't know how to thank you. Is it from all of you or just from Tom?"

"It's from me," Tom grinned. "Beth helped pick it out. She thought you'd like it."

"I love it! Please put it on, Tom."

Tom's hands were rough and scarred from his job at the factory, but he managed to slip the ring through the tiny catch. He looked as proud as Punch when Bayley ran to a full-length mirror to see how she looked in his gift.

Now she was full of chatter. "Is that why you asked me to wear this dress, Dad? How come you're all making such a fuss? It isn't my birthday or anything."

"You've been kind of good to all of us this summer," her father said, and the others nodded agreement.

"Maybe, but not this good. I don't deserve anything like this."

"That's not for you to say," he told her.

The waiter ushered them to the terrace overlooking the formal gardens, where their table was set. The boys all rushed to pull out Bayley's chair, but the waiter got there first. He and Chip banged their heads together in the process, and that broke the ice and the Hughes family began to relax.

Chip relaxed the atmosphere further, with his struggles with the menu. They were all trying to puzzle out what the French phrases meant when Chip asked plaintively, "Where's the hamburger sandwiches?"

"No!" Benjy exploded. "He can't ask for a hamburger sandwich in a place like this!"

"I don't see anything on this program to eat," Chip protested.

"I guess Chip's right. We need some professional assistance," their father said, and beckoned to the waiter. This character had lost his aloofness after he cracked heads with Chip, and now he patiently went down the menu, translating the French terms into food. It took some time, but at last they all succeeded in ordering what they wanted. Bayley settled for pheasant, because this sounded like the most exotic item.

She sipped her water and looked around. Many of the women wore dinner clothes, but her simple yellow dress looked all right, especially with Tom's pendant.

She noticed that her father was signaling Chip with his eyebrows. "Oh yeah," Chip said. He tried to imitate Tom's casual way of presenting a gift. "Bay, here's a little something from me, on account of you haven't been so terribly horrible to us this summer."

Bayley opened the tiny box. A pair of amethyst earrings of the same clear, dark purple as her pendant rested on the cotton. Benjy said quickly, "Bay, don't turn on the water works, or everybody will think we're a bunch of creeps at this table."

"They cost five dollars," Chip informed her. "Boy, did I have a time getting it up!"

Bayley managed to suppress her desire to jump up and kiss Chip, whose earnest sincerity shone in his face.

The shrimp cocktails came then, and Chip was so intrigued by the elaborate service he had them all laughing, until one of his shrimps got away from him and jumped from its nest of ice into the bowl of flowers in the middle of the table. Benjy snarled under his breath that Chip ought to eat out of Happy's dish at home, because Happy had better manners than he did. Bayley snarled back that her twin ought to shut his face and leave his brother alone, because it wasn't Chip's fault; the shrimp was slippery.

Benjy didn't take offense. The waiter removed the plates and brought salad and rolls. Chip began happily exploring the varieties of rolls, but the others seemed uneasy. Finally Mr. Hughes chuckled. "We had a program planned, Bayley," he said. "Chip's earrings were to come with the first course; Benjy's gift, with the next; mine, with the last. But we can't wait any longer."

"You don't mean there are more presents! But why, why?"

Benjy pulled his gift out of his pocket. "I'd have had it wrapped nicer if you hadn't gotten snoopy and barged in when I was trying to find some ribbon in Mother's closet," he explained.

For a moment, Bayley didn't recognize what it was. Then she saw it was a sweater guard, with small cut amethysts at either end. It wasn't showy, but graceful and delicate, like Tom's pendant. "Stay where you are!" Benjy ordered fiercely. "Don't you try to kiss me!"

"But how am I going to thank you?" Bayley asked helplessly.

"Dad, give her yours now," Tom said. "This stringing it out is just getting her all worked up. If she's going to have hysterics, she might as well have 'em all at once."

Her father handed Bayley the smallest box of all. While she fumbled with the paper, she guessed what it was. It could only be a ring.

She pushed the catch and the top shot up. Nestled in white velvet was a pale, enormous amethyst, cut brilliant style. "It's a real ring," Bayley said stupidly.

She slipped it on her finger, and it fitted. "That's a break," her father said. "I had to guess at the size. Do you like it, kitten?"

"Like it? Like it?" Bayley choked.

183

"Wear it," Benjy told her, as she started to put it back in its box.

"I never had a ring before. I never had jewels," Bayley said. "I never had nice earrings or a necklace with a real stone, and I never even hoped to have a guard like that to wear with the cashmere sweater Dad gave me last Christmas. But why, why? Why did you do all this?"

Chip explained for all of them. "We thought we ought to reward you," he said. "You probably wanted to poison us all summer, but you never did."

"Yes, and I don't know why I didn't," Bayley said. "I certainly had some neat chances."

The White Fox Inn lived up to expectations. The dinner was a never-to-be-forgotten experience, and the combination of soft music and delicious food and the flower scent from the gardens below the terrace gave the evening a dreamlike quality.

While Mr. Hughes was paying the bill, Benjy got a look at it and exclaimed, "Yipes!" That brought them down to earth. He yipped again when his older brother corrected him with a punch in the ribs.

Afterward, they walked in the gardens, and then they went home.

Bayley tried a dozen times to say, "Thank you," but they wouldn't let her.

"That's all right, Bay," Tom told her.

"Yeah, you'd better shut up, Bay," her twin said. "You'd only get sloppy and mess up your mascara or something."

184

"I haven't got any mascara on!"

"Yeah? What's that dark stuff under your eyes, then? Dirt?"

"I washed my face!"

"Listen, with a face like yours, washing's not enough. Did you ever think of sand-blasting?"

The bickering went on all the way home, and Mr. Hughes didn't try to stop it.

He followed Bayley up to her room, when she had said good night and left them. She was taking off her new jewels, putting each item in its own box.

"Daughter, the boys asked me to tell you that if you want to change any of the things, it's all right with them," he said. "We got the idea it would be fun to buy you a complete outfit, but it does seem like a lot of purple. We told the jeweler you might want to change them, so if you go to the store he'll be expecting you."

Bayley sat on the edge of her bed, her treasures in her lap. She felt the cool smoothness of the stones, then rubbed them to make them shiny again. "No," she said, "I adore the color. I still wish I knew why you all did it, though. I don't deserve it. I never appreciated my brothers before, and that's a terrible thing to say.

"I love it because they match, Daddy. I'll wear them together all my life, because each thing is one of you. I guess I'll always think of this summer as sort of an amethyst time. I don't want to get sloppy, but it's hard not to, because I wanted a real ring terribly badly. And the other things . . ." Her voice trailed off.

Her father hugged her, holding her hard against him. Then he left her alone.

Bayley put each piece of jewelry in its own box, but left the covers off. After she had turned off her light, the moonlight illuminated her familiar room, and a pale shaft shone directly on the boxes set in a row on the night table near her pillow. The moonlight caught lavender fire in the amethyst stones.

Bayley lay on her side and watched this light and thought back on the long days of the summer now coming to an end. She thought solemn thoughts that were too complicated to put into words, and finally she sleepily giggled, alone in the dark. Jeepers, she thought, I'm rich. I bet I feel like Mrs. Kidd used to, when Cap'n Kidd came home with a good haul. Then she went to sleep.